"Dogs look up to us. Cats look down on us. Pigs treat us as equals."

—Winston Churchill

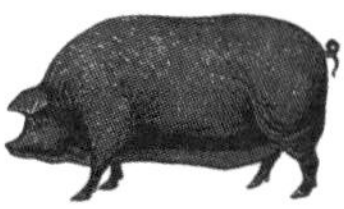

"...the thing about reptiles is that they really just wanna be left alone, and I understand them."

—Nicholas Cage

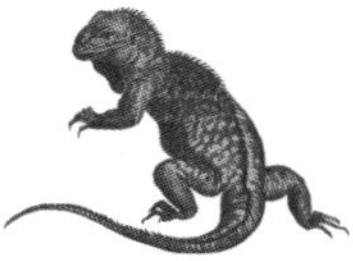

PUBLISHED BY TOP SHELF PRODUCTIONS, AN IMPRINT OF IDW PUBLISHING, A DIVISION OF IDEA AND DESIGN WORKS, LLC. OFFICES: TOP SHELF PRODUCTIONS, C/O IDEA & DESIGN WORKS, LLC, 2355 NORTHSIDE DRIVE, SUITE 140, SAN DIEGO, CA 92108.

PRINTED IN KOREA.
EDITOR-IN-CHIEF: CHRIS STAROS.

ISBN: 978-1-60309-523-5   26 25 24 23   1 2 3 4

VISIT OUR ONLINE CATALOG AT TOPSHELFCOMIX.COM.

This is a story that starts when THIS pot-bellied pig

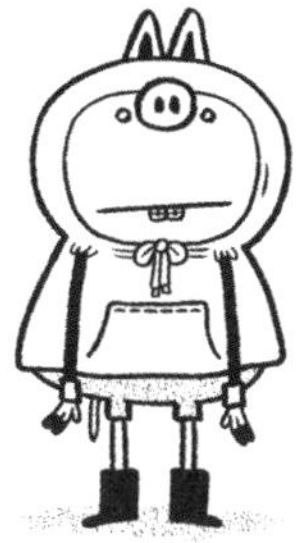

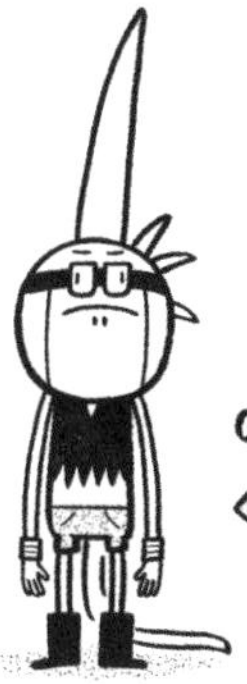

and THIS iguana

drive a miniature train through the front gate of THIS petting zoo.

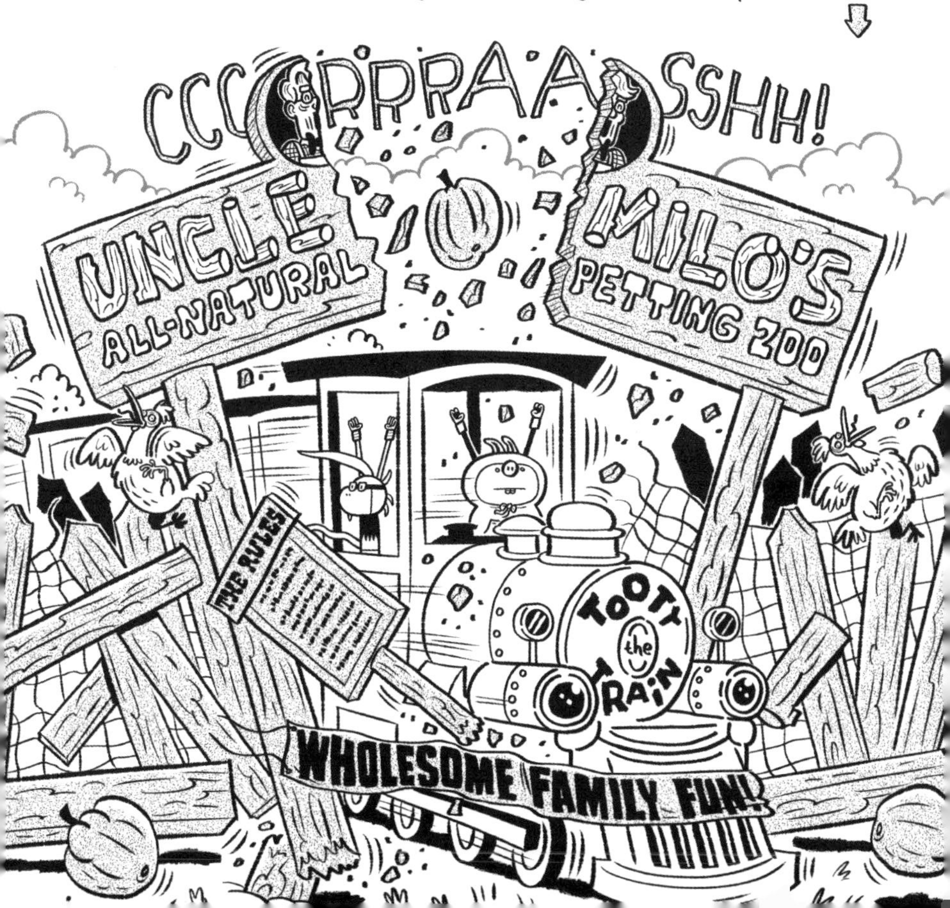
CCCRRRAAASSHH!
UNCLE MILO'S
ALL-NATURAL PETTING ZOO
THE RULES!
TOOTY the TRAIN
WHOLESOME FAMILY FUN!

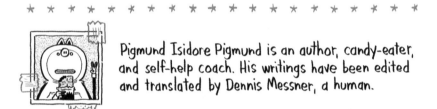

Pigmund Isidore Pigmund is an author, candy-eater, and self-help coach. His writings have been edited and translated by Dennis Messner, a human.

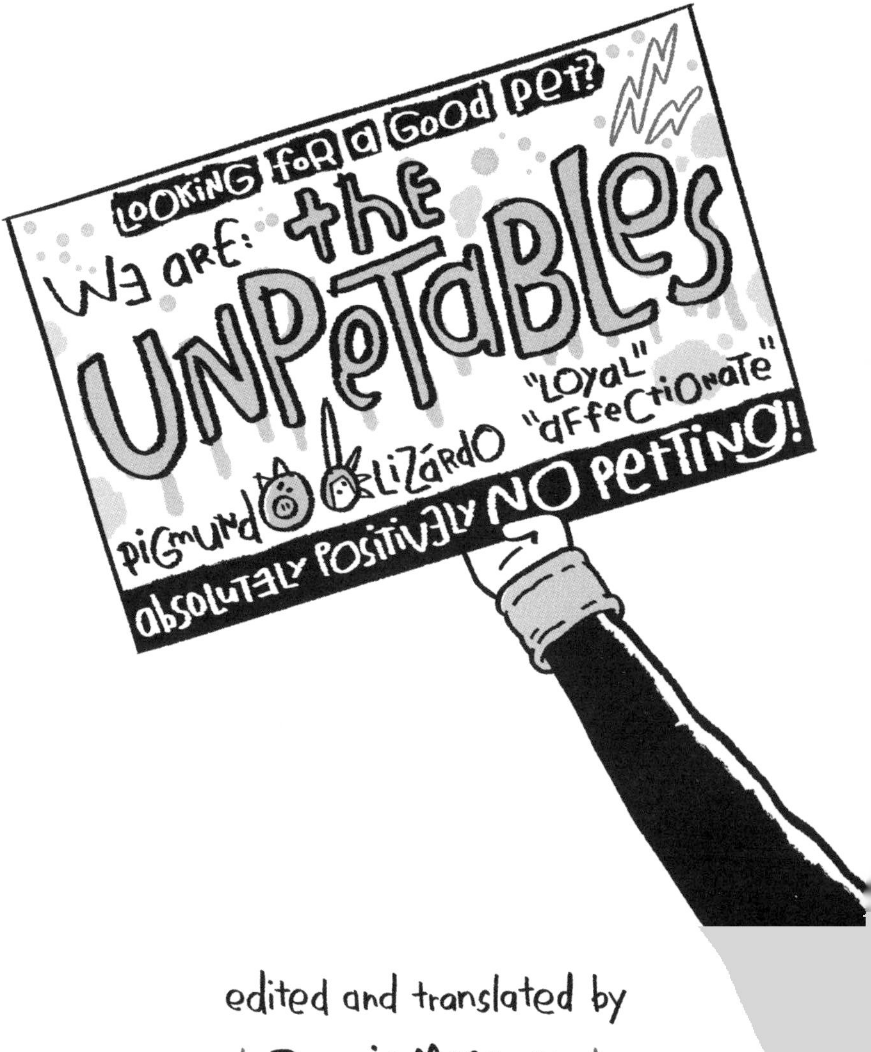
LOOKING FOR A GOOD PET?
WE ARE:
THE UNPETABLES
PIGMUND
LIZÁRDO
"LOYAL"
"AFFECTIONATE"
ABSOLUTELY POSITIVELY NO PETTING!

edited and translated by

★ Dennis Messner ★

Adventure 1

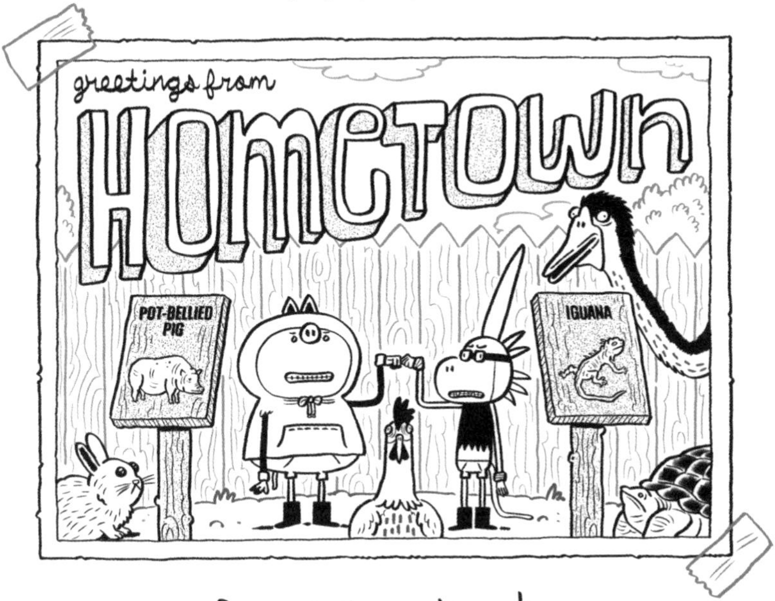
greetings from
HOMETOWN
POT-BELLIED PIG
IGUANA

Escape From Paradise

Let me explain that whole train thingy.

My name is Pigmund.

My recorded place of birth is Uncle Milo's All-Natural Petting Zoo.

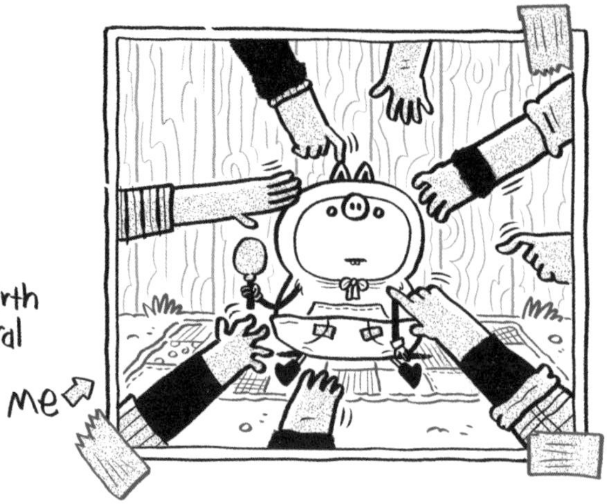
Me

Growing up in a petting zoo was definitely NOT easy. But at an early age, I began writing my life story on the back of used paper plates.

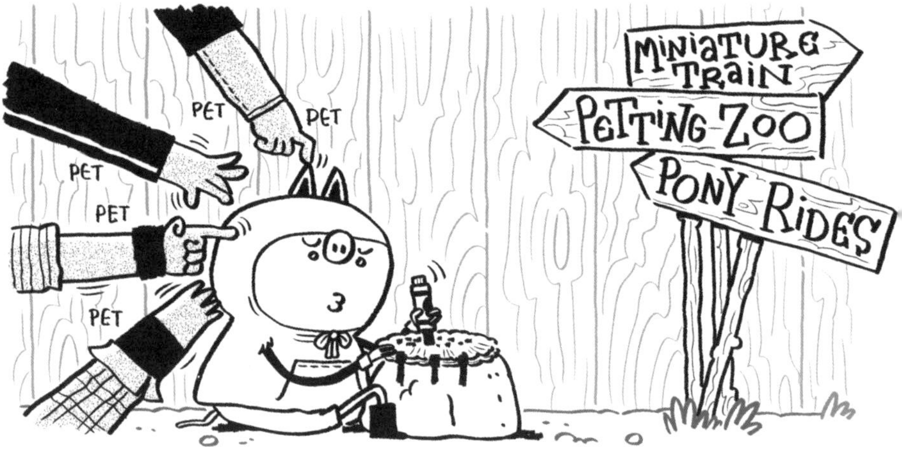
PET
PET
PET
PET
PET
MINIATURE TRAIN
PETTING ZOO
PONY RIDES

I call this great work of art "The Paper Plate Diaries." And you're reading it RIGHT NOW.

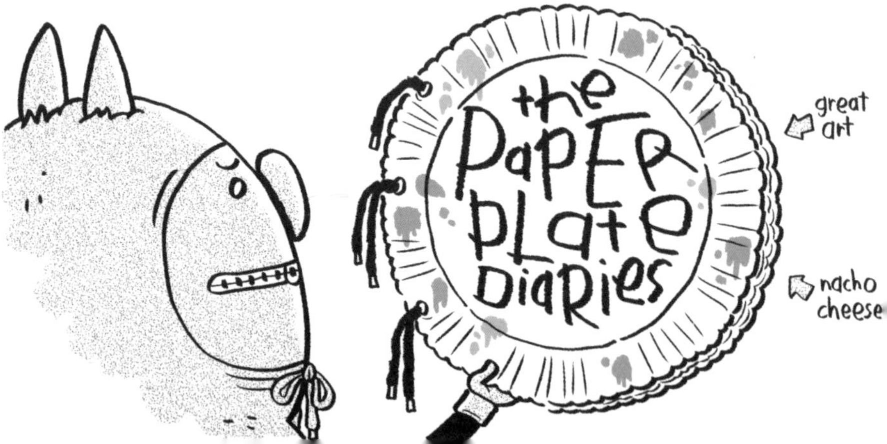
the Paper plate diaries
great art
nacho cheese

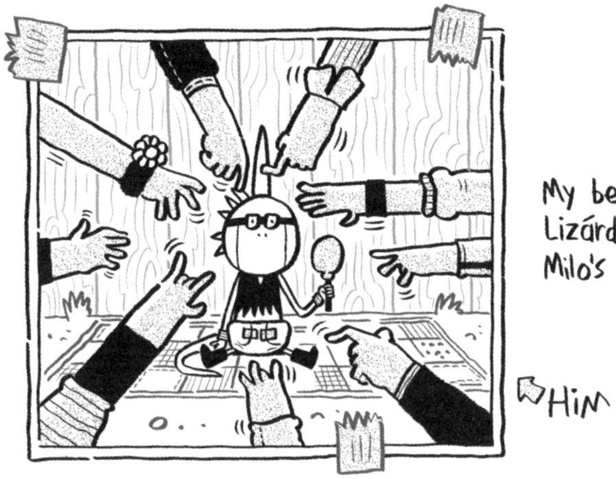
HIM

My best friend is a lizard.
Lizárdo was also born in Uncle Milo's All-Natural Petting Zoo.

I won't lie.
Lizárdo doesn't have a whole lot of common sense.

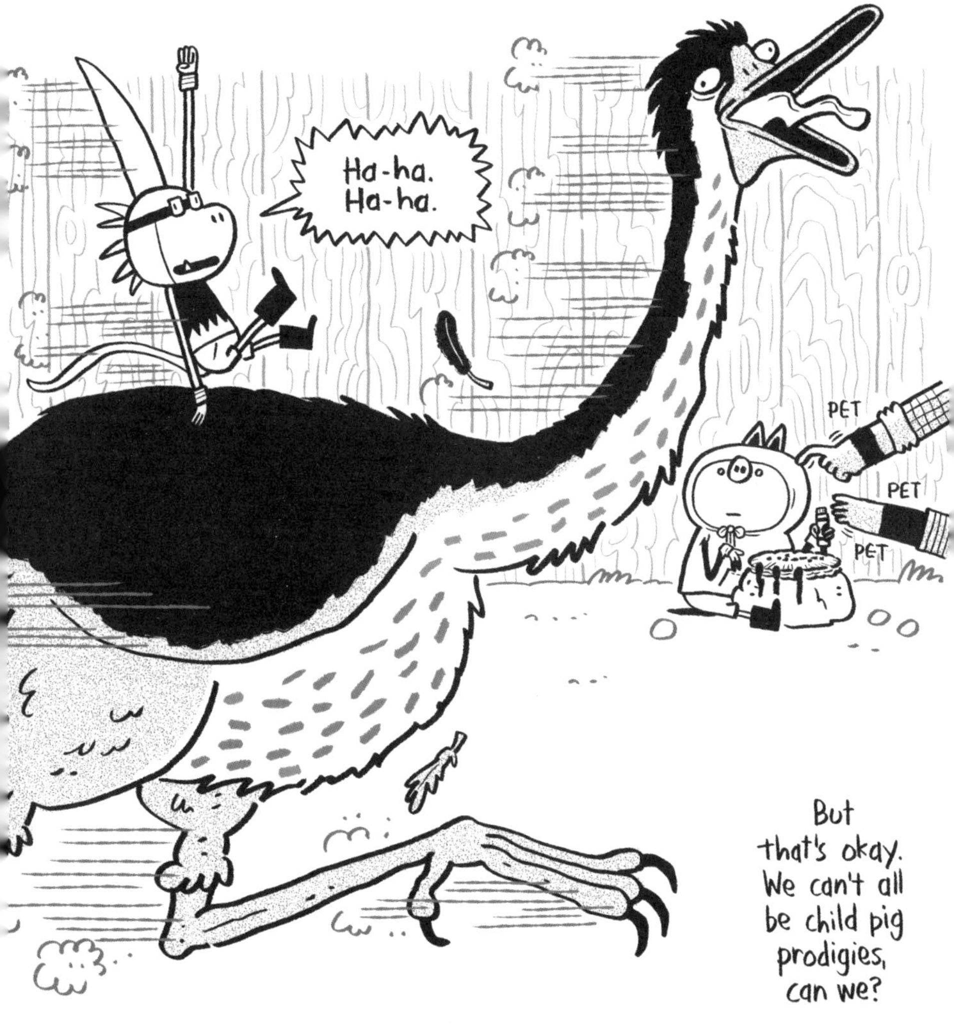
Ha-ha. Ha-ha.
PET
PET
PET
But that's okay. We can't all be child pig prodigies, can we?

This is Maintenance Man Kenny, the maintenance man at Uncle Milo's All-Natural Petting Zoo.

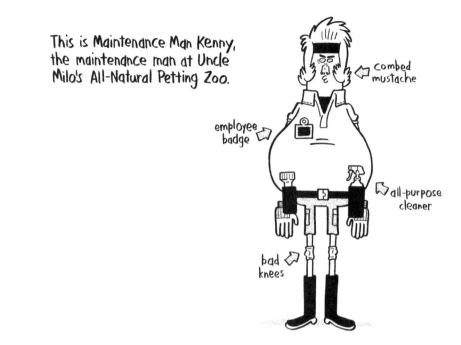

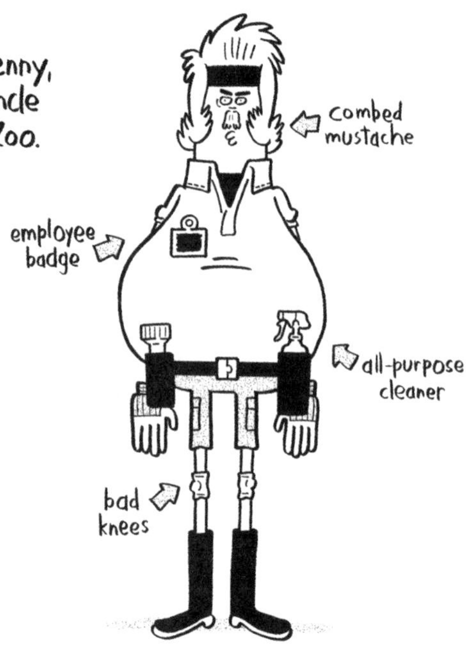
combed mustache
employee badge
all-purpose cleaner
bad knees

And this is Maintenance Man Kenny in his electric maintenance cart chasing me and my best friend Lizárdo. That's because after me and my best friend Lizárdo drove that miniature train through the front gate of Uncle Milo's All-Natural Petting Zoo, we made our escape on getaway chickens.

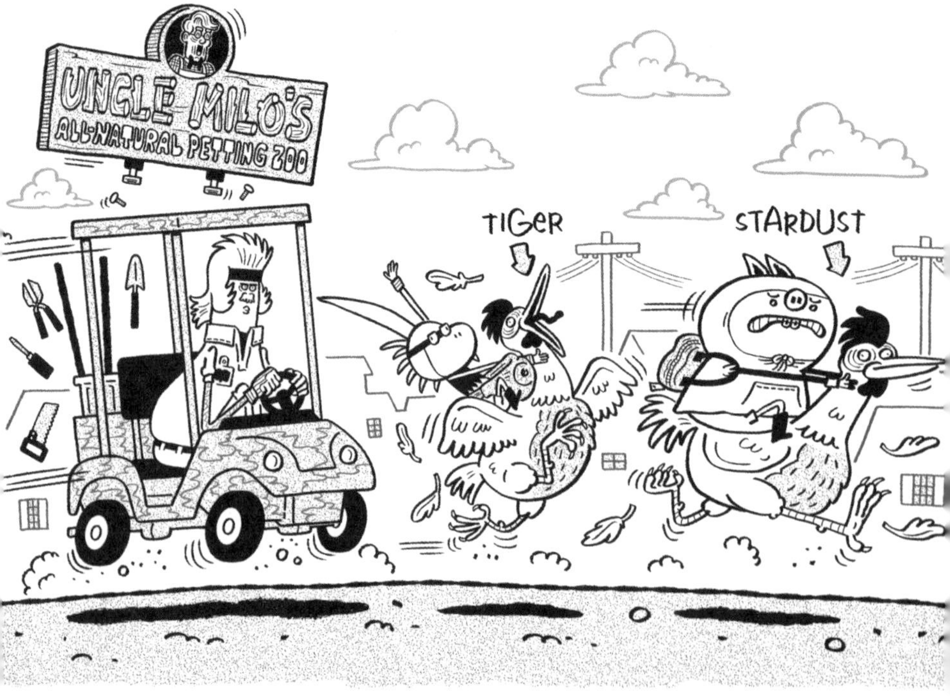
UNCLE MILO'S
ALL-NATURAL PETTING ZOO
TIGER
STARDUST

I have a full name. It is PIGMUND ISIDORE PIGMUND.

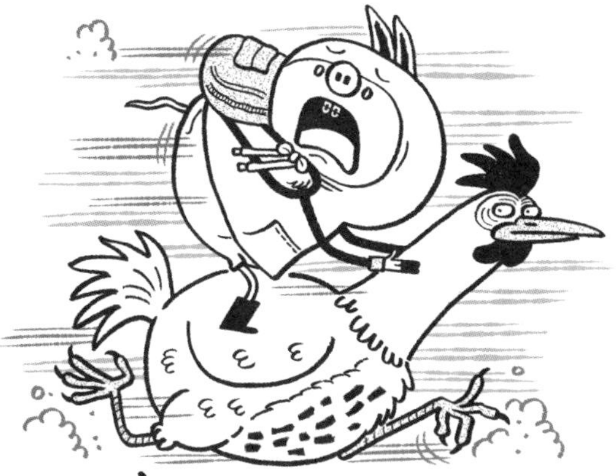

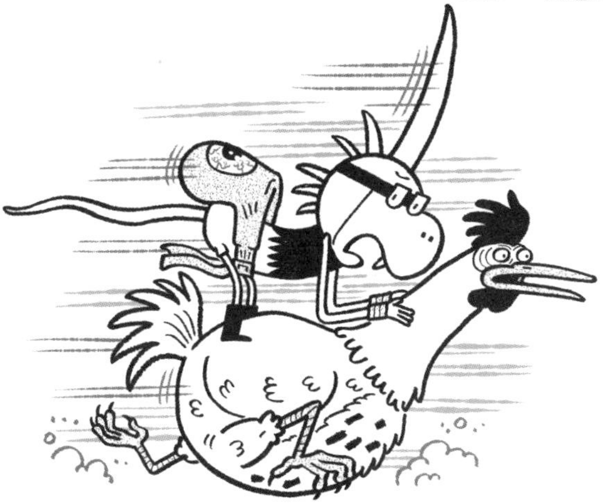

Lizárdo also has a full name. It is LIZÁRDO VAN BUREN VAN HALEN.

"You can't outrun Maintenance Man Kenny, Uncle Milo's loyal and faithful servant!"

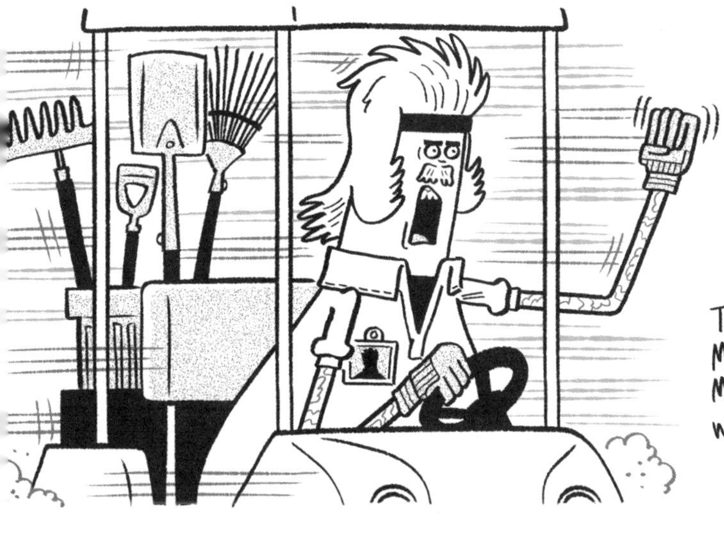

That was Maintenance Man Kenny who said that.

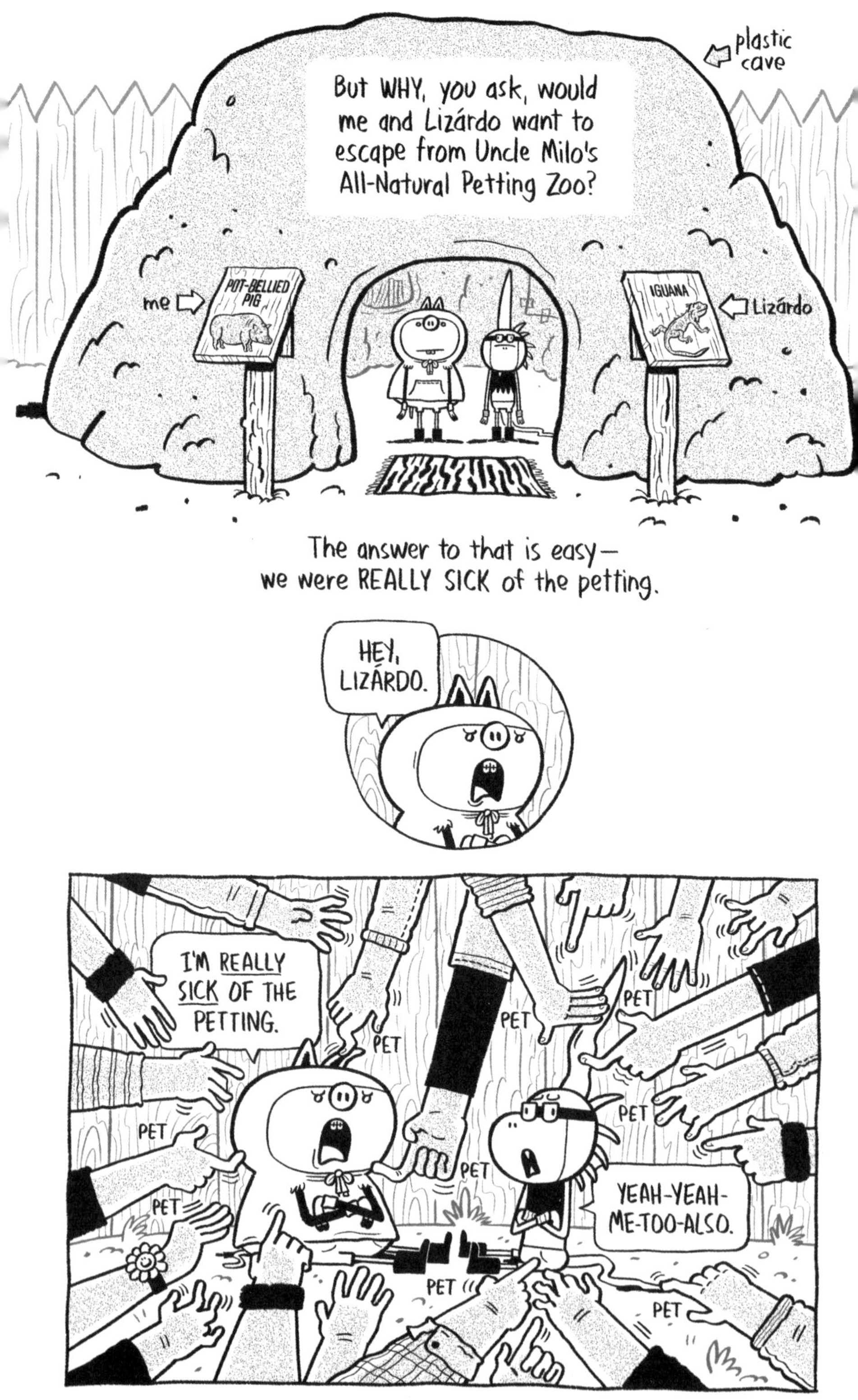
plastic cave
But WHY, you ask, would me and Lizárdo want to escape from Uncle Milo's All-Natural Petting Zoo?
me
POT-BELLIED PIG
IGUANA
Lizárdo
The answer to that is easy— we were REALLY SICK of the petting.
HEY, LIZÁRDO.
I'M REALLY SICK OF THE PETTING.
PET
PET
PET
PET
PET
PET
PET
PET
YEAH-YEAH-ME-TOO-ALSO.
PET

And so, after LOTS of failed escape attempts,

me and the lizard used some plastic spoons to dig a tunnel into Tooty the Train's Train Station.

SLAP, SLAP, SLAP, SLAP, SLAP, SLAP, SLAP, SLAP, SLAP, SLAP, SLAP, SLAP, SLAP, SLAP, SLAP,

Then, after a slight disagreement over who got to drive Tooty,

we CHOO-CHOO-CHOOED into Freedom.

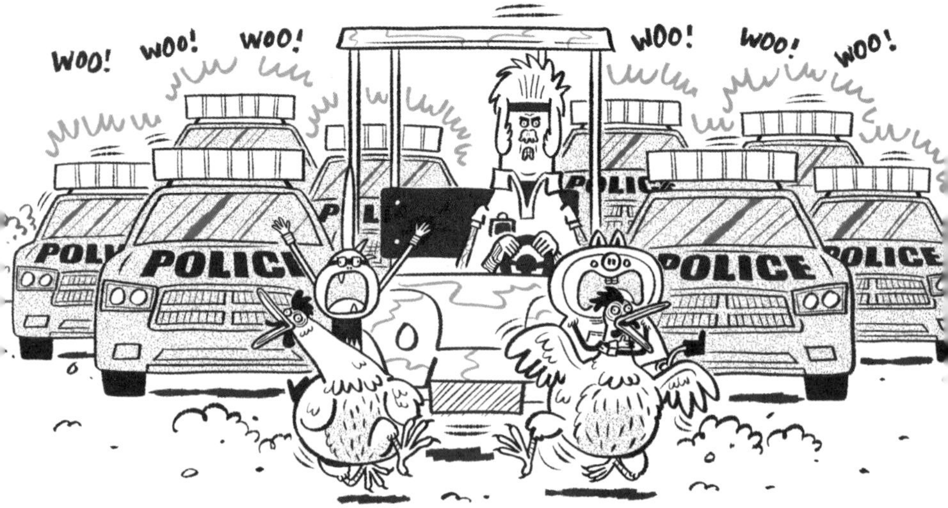
WOO! WOO! WOO!
WOO! WOO! WOO!
POLICE
POLICE
POLICE

Oh. I forgot to tell you about our exciting, action-packed, high-speed chase. Never mind. That'll take too much explaining.

"The runaway pig and igauna just ran past that DANGER: BRIDGE OUT sign! They're trapped!"

That was Maintenance Man Kenny again.

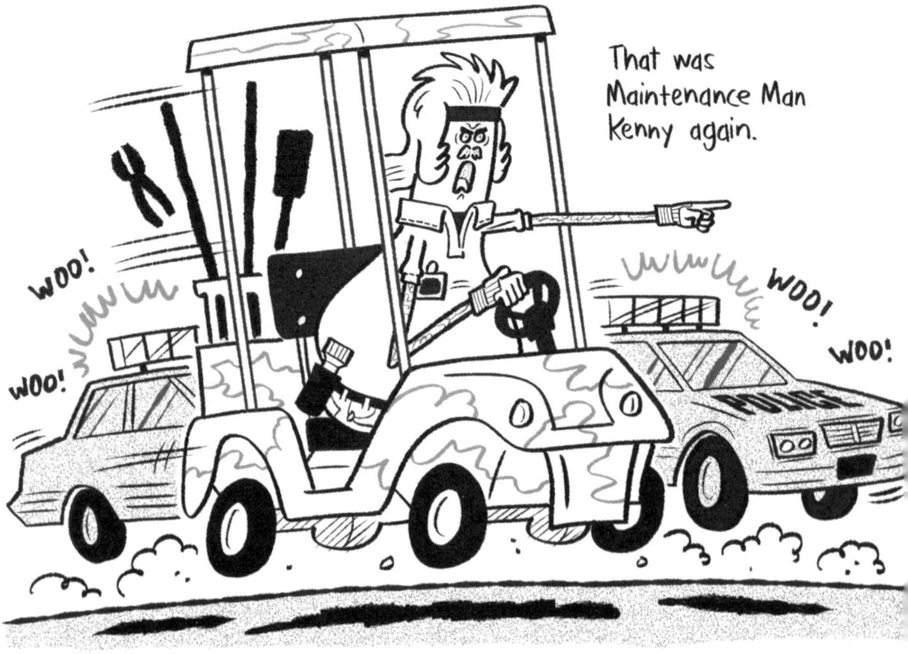
WOO!
WOO!
WOO!
WOO!
POLICE

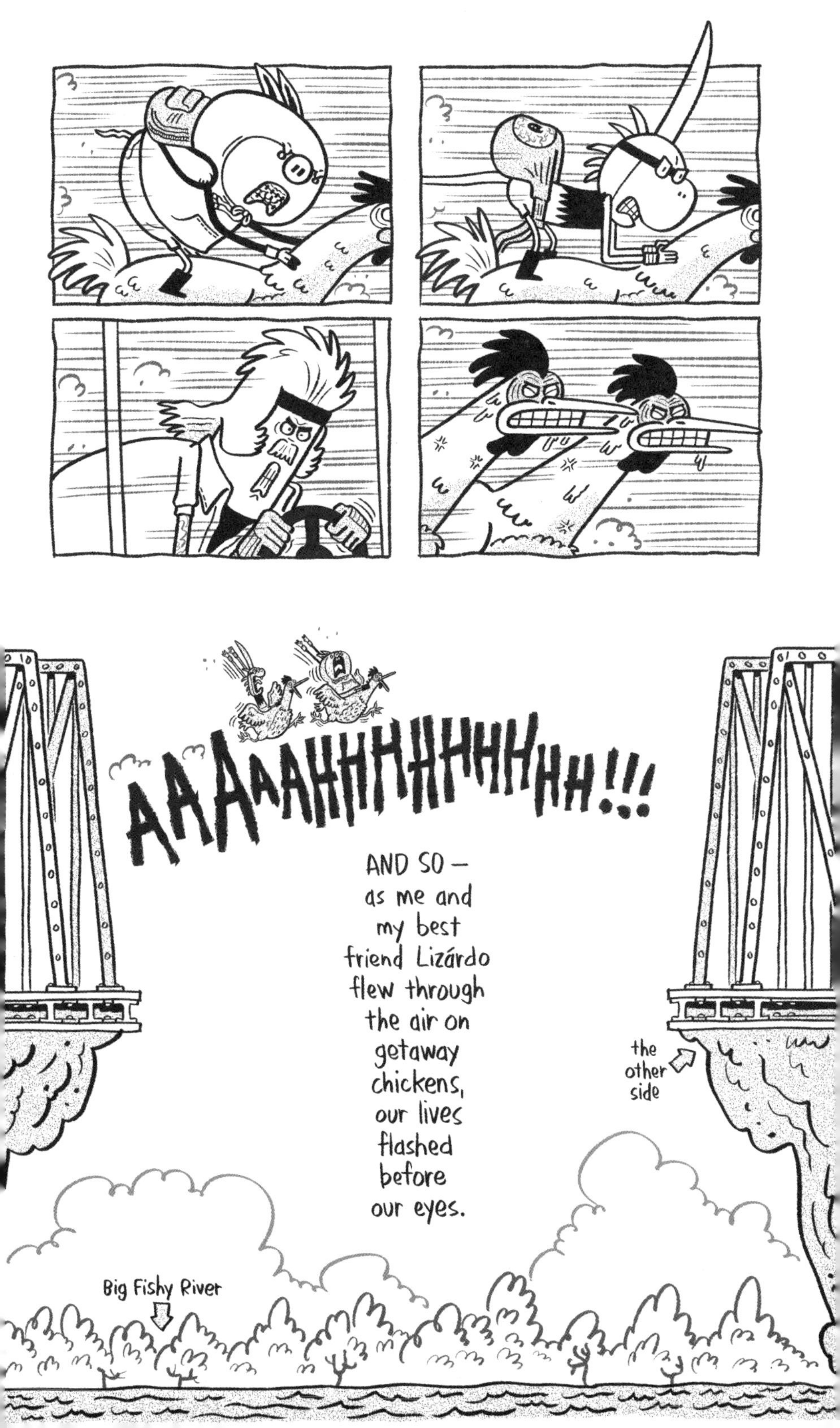
AAAAAHHHHHHHHHH!!!
AND SO — as me and my best friend Lizárdo flew through the air on getaway chickens, our lives flashed before our eyes.
the other side
Big Fishy River

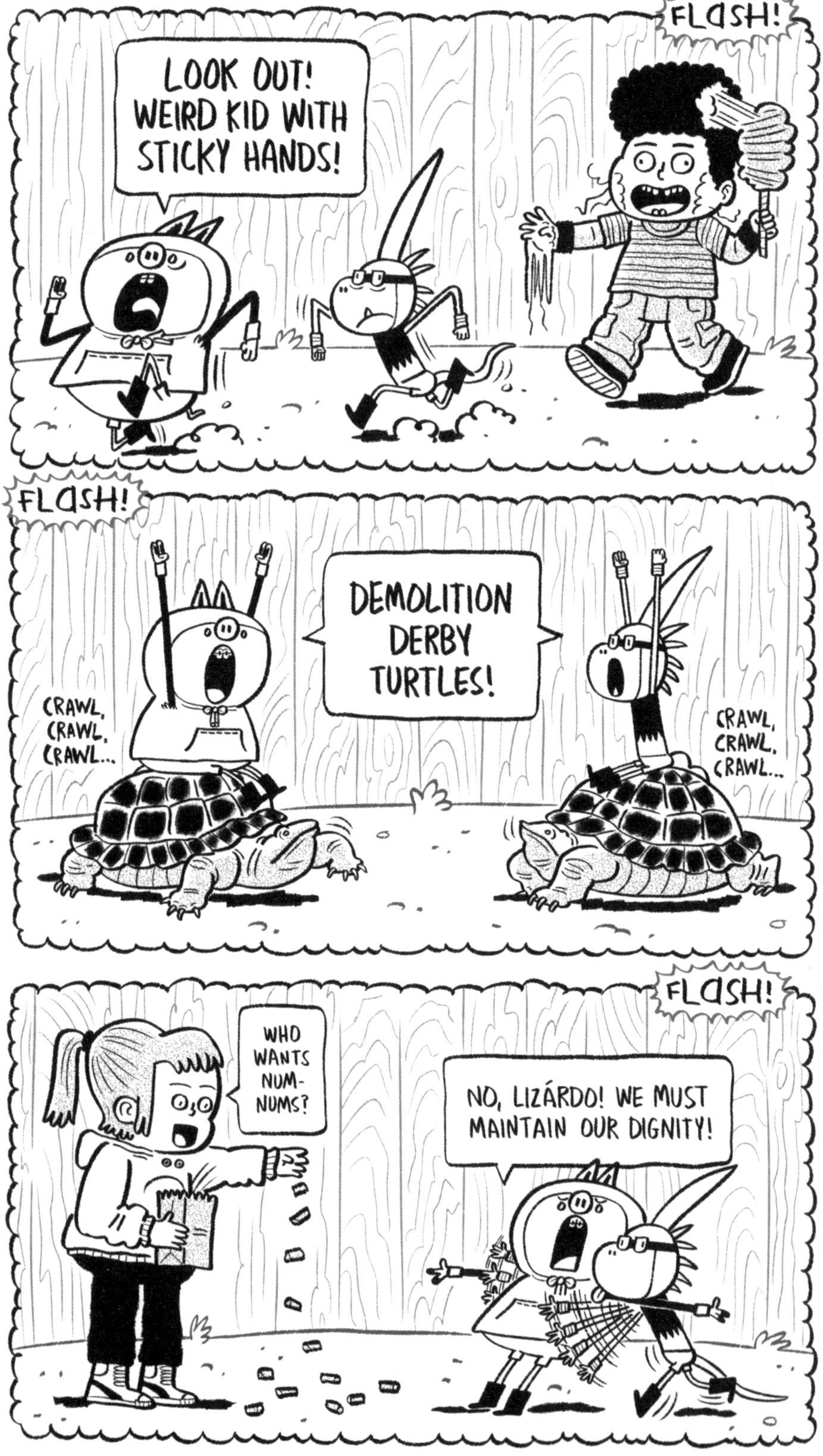
FLASH!
LOOK OUT! WEIRD KID WITH STICKY HANDS!
FLASH!
CRAWL, CRAWL, CRAWL...
DEMOLITION DERBY TURTLES!
CRAWL, CRAWL, CRAWL...
FLASH!
WHO WANTS NUM-NUMS?
NO, LIZÁRDO! WE MUST MAINTAIN OUR DIGNITY!

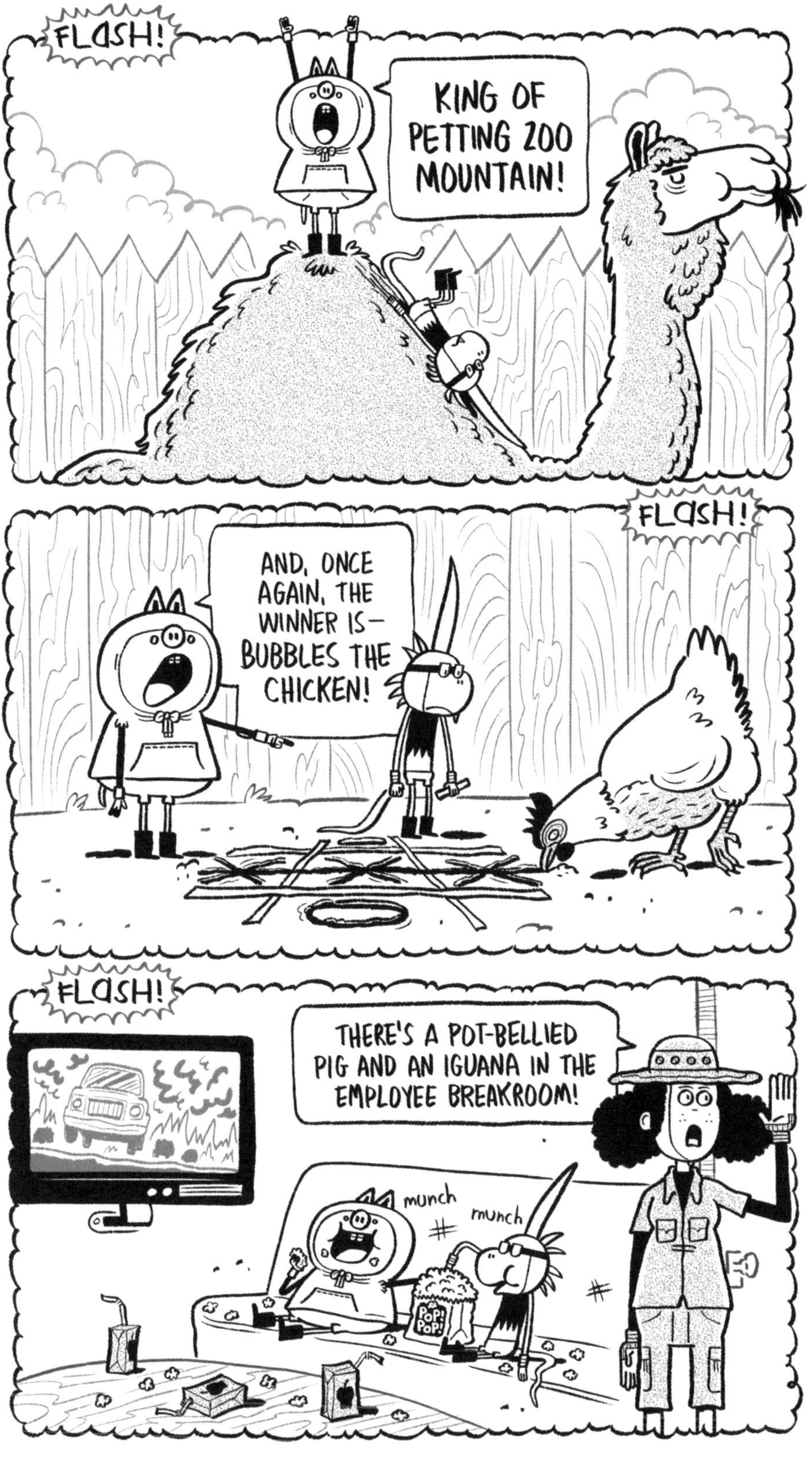
FLASH!
KING OF PETTING ZOO MOUNTAIN!
FLASH!
AND, ONCE AGAIN, THE WINNER IS—BUBBLES THE CHICKEN!
FLASH!
THERE'S A POT-BELLIED PIG AND AN IGUANA IN THE EMPLOYEE BREAKROOM!
munch
munch
POP! POP!

HEY, LOOK. ⇨
While me and my best friend Lizárdo's lives were flashing before our eyes, Tiger and Stardust landed safely on the other side.

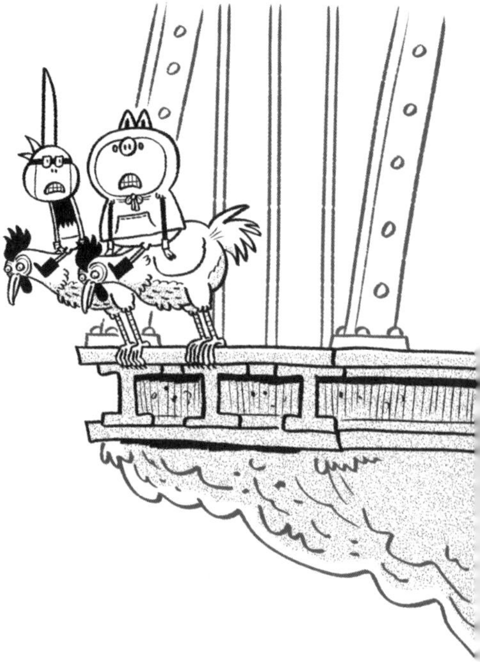

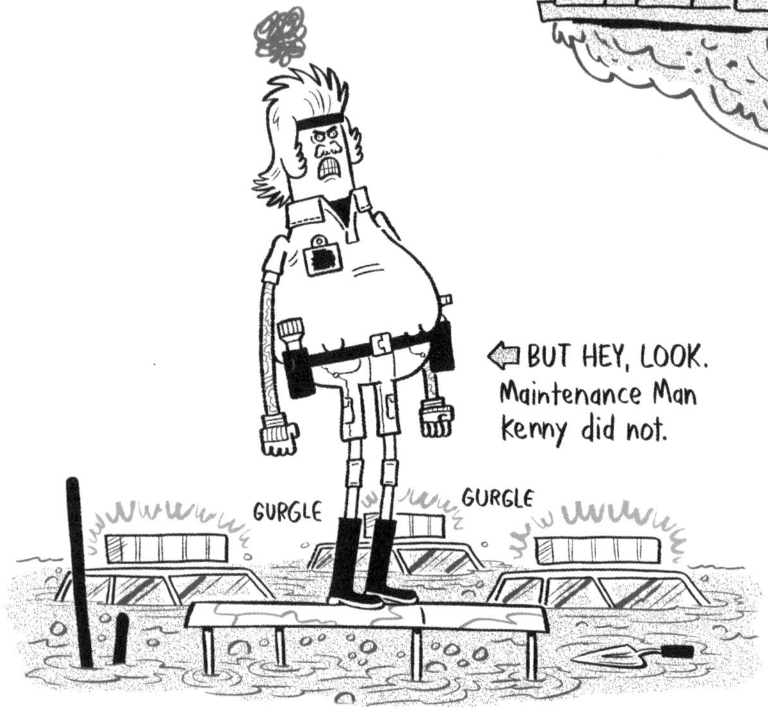
GURGLE
GURGLE

⇦ BUT HEY, LOOK.
Maintenance Man Kenny did not.

"No one gets out of Uncle Milo's All-Natural Petting Zoo!" yelled the slowly sinking maintenance man.

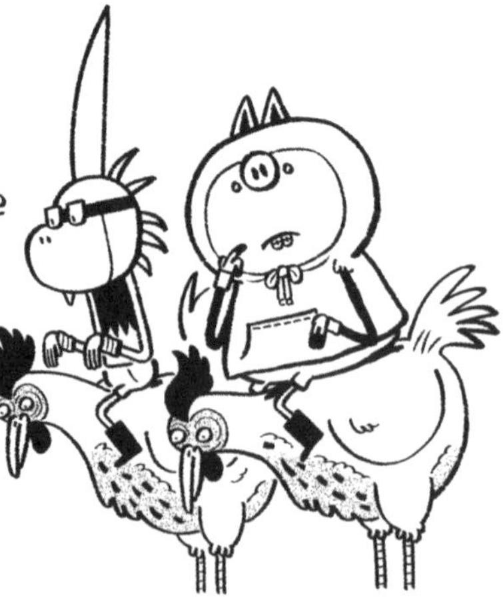

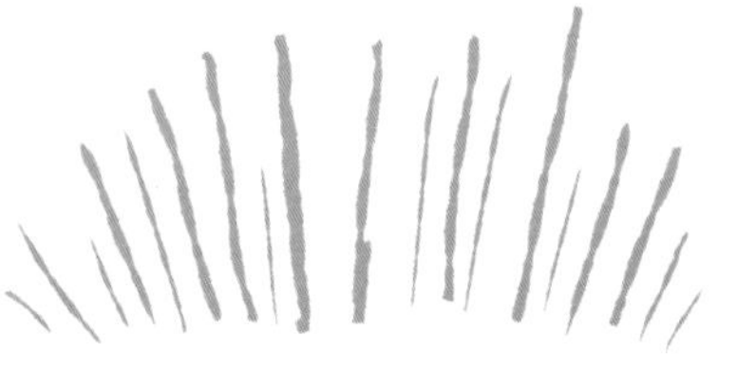

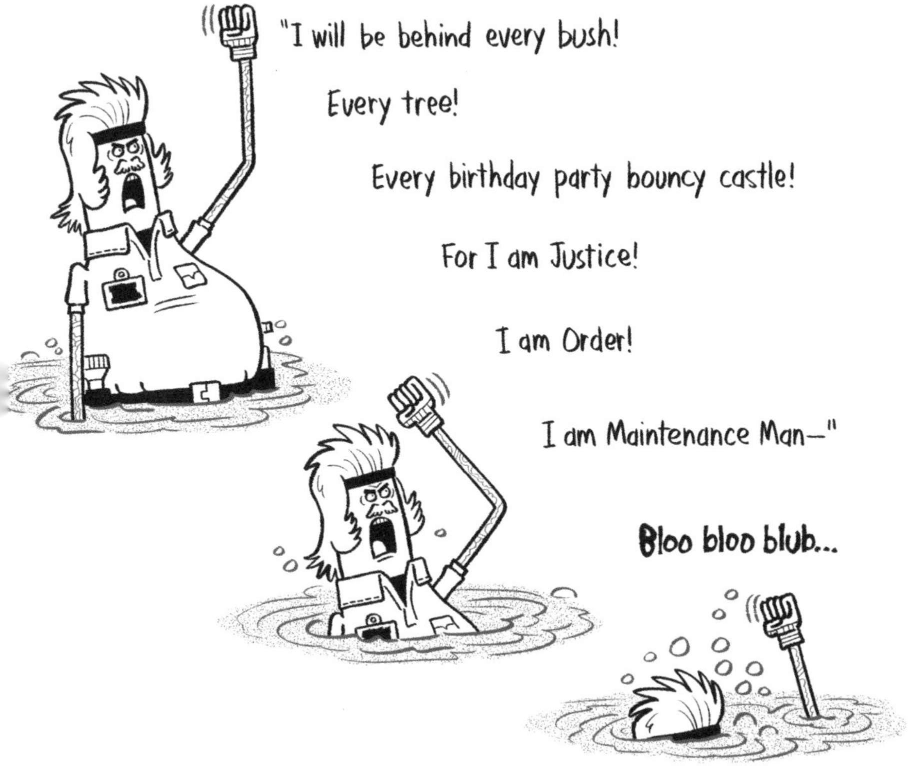
"I will be behind every bush!
Every tree!
Every birthday party bouncy castle!
For I am Justice!
I am Order!
I am Maintenance Man—"
Bloo bloo blub...

And with that bloo-bloo-blub, me and Lizárdo had escaped the sticky hands of about a zillion little kids. With that bloo-bloo-blub, me and Lizárdo were FREE and INDEPENDENT pets.

And this is where our EPIC, MONUMENTAL, very large adventures BEGIN.

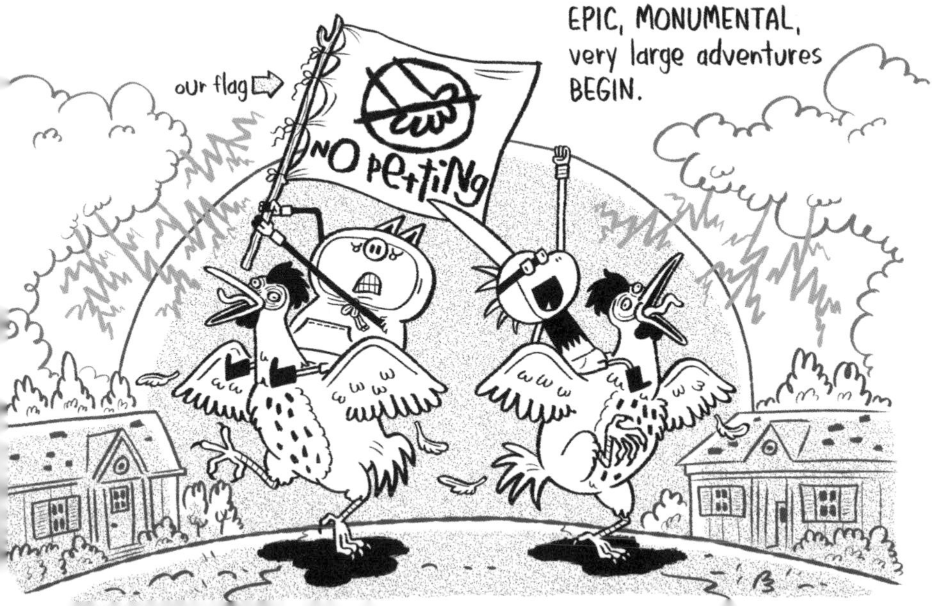
our flag
NO PETTING

Adventure 2

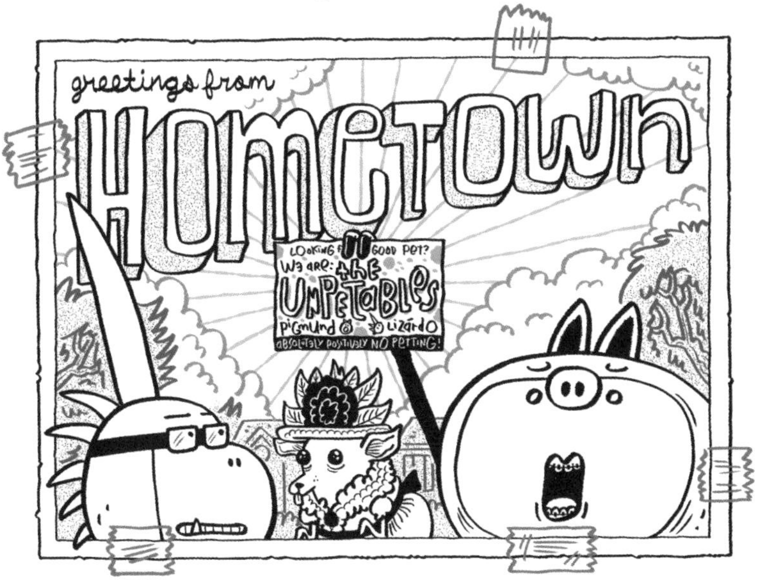
greetings from
HOMETOWN
LOOKING FOR A GOOD PET?
WE ARE: the
UNPETABLES
pigmund
lizardo
ABSOLUTELY POSITIVELY NO PETTING!

How To Declare Independence (Without Even Trying)

About me!

STORY OF A CHILD PIG PRODIGY

STOP EVERYTHING. I gotta tell you a little bit about ME. I, Pigmund Isidore Pigmund, was born a POT-BELLIED PIG. But, to be honest, I don't particularly care for that word POT-BELLIED.

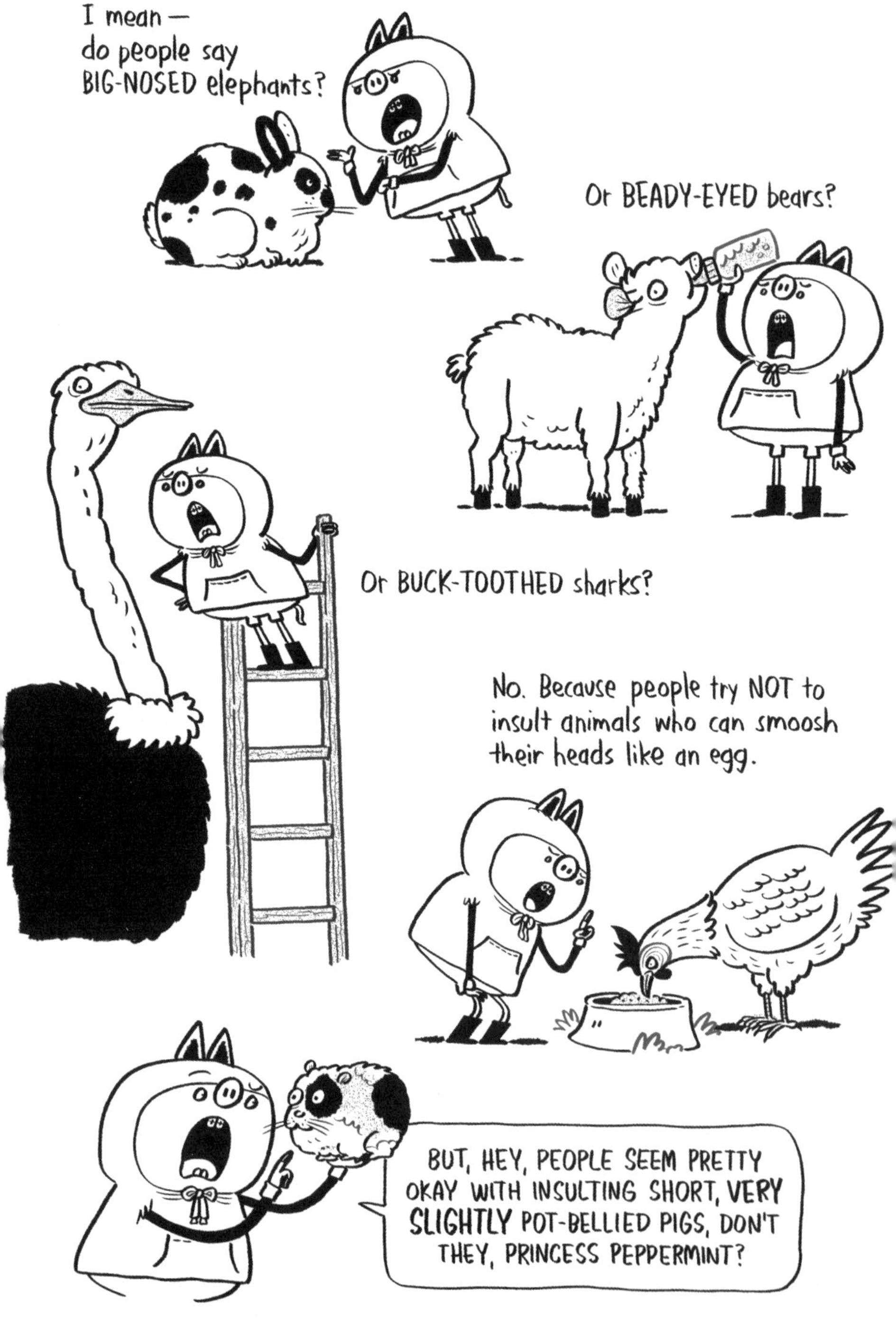

I mean — do people say BIG-NOSED elephants?
Or BEADY-EYED bears?
Or BUCK-TOOTHED sharks?
No. Because people try NOT to insult animals who can smoosh their heads like an egg.
BUT, HEY, PEOPLE SEEM PRETTY OKAY WITH INSULTING SHORT, VERY SLIGHTLY POT-BELLIED PIGS, DON'T THEY, PRINCESS PEPPERMINT?

Here's something you don't know about me. While Lizárdo was finishing up that tunnel to Tooty the Train's Train Station, I was writing a DECLARATION OF INDEPENDENCE on the back of a used paper plate.

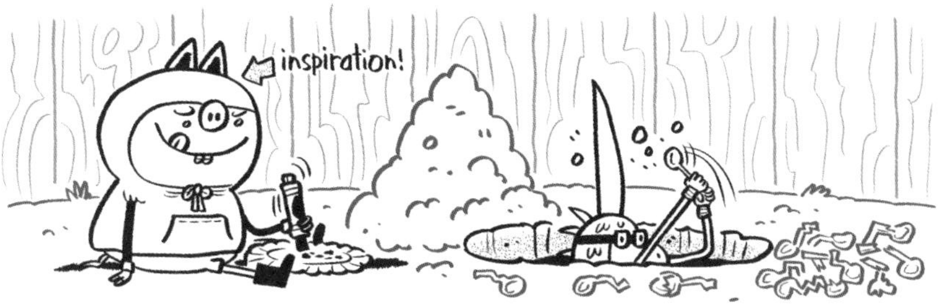
inspiration!

Then, right before we escaped from Uncle Milo's All-Natural Petting Zoo, I glued that historical document to the door of Maintenance Man Kenny's tool shed.

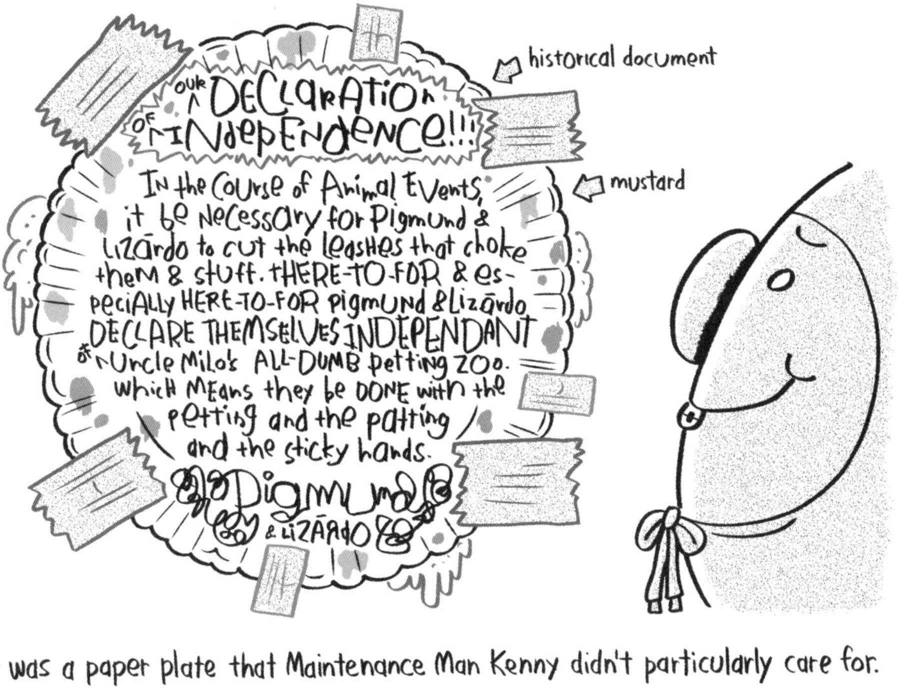
historical document
our DECLARATION of INDEPENDENCE!!!
In the Course of Animal Events, it be Necessary for Pigmund & Lizárdo to cut the leashes that choke them & stuff. THERE-TO-FOR & especially HERE-TO-FOR Pigmund & Lizárdo DECLARE THEMSELVES INDEPENDANT of Uncle Milo's ALL-DUMB petting ZOO. which Means they be DONE with the petting and the patting and the sticky hands.
Pigmund
& Lizárdo
mustard

It was a paper plate that Maintenance Man Kenny didn't particularly care for.

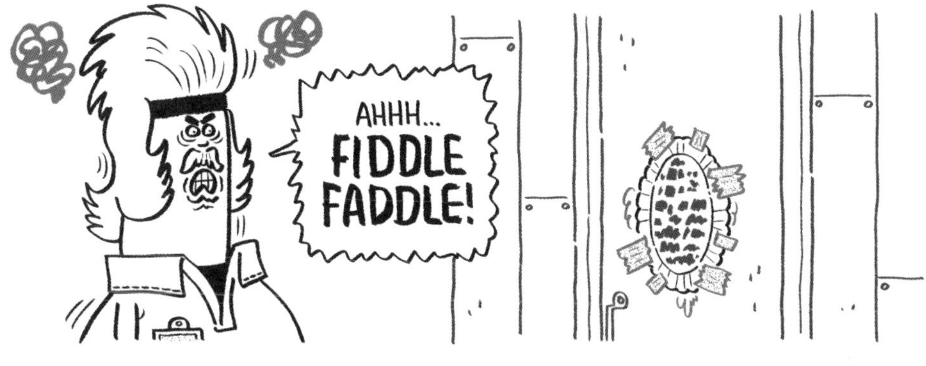
AHHH...
FIDDLE FADDLE!

STORY OF A LIZARD BOY

Now a little bit about Lizárdo. Lizárdo was born an IGUANA. But that fact may be a LIE. Because a little while later, Zookeeper Jesse said:

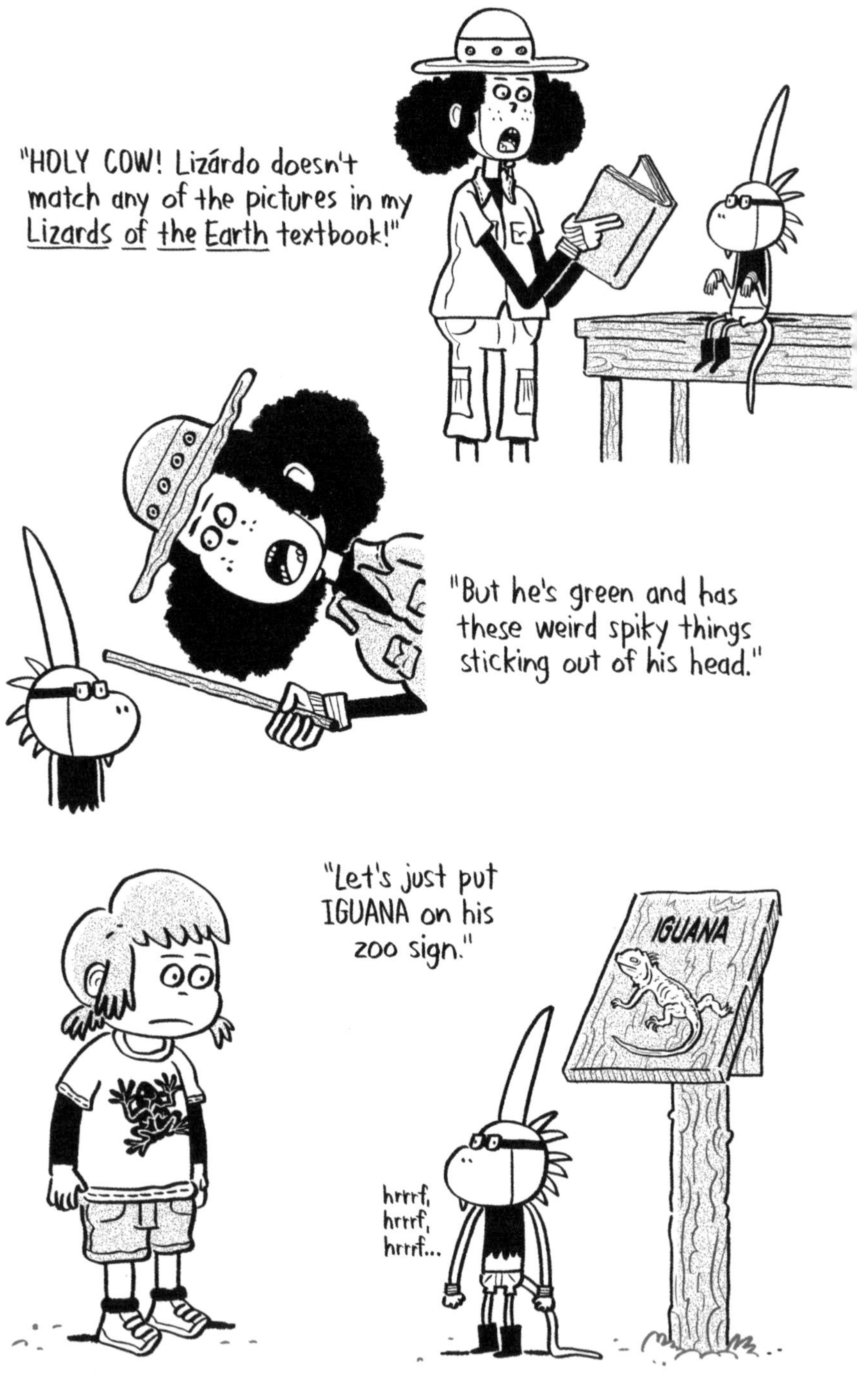
"HOLY COW! Lizárdo doesn't match any of the pictures in my Lizards of the Earth textbook!"
"But he's green and has these weird spiky things sticking out of his head."
"Let's just put IGUANA on his zoo sign."
IGUANA
hrrrf, hrrrf, hrrrf...

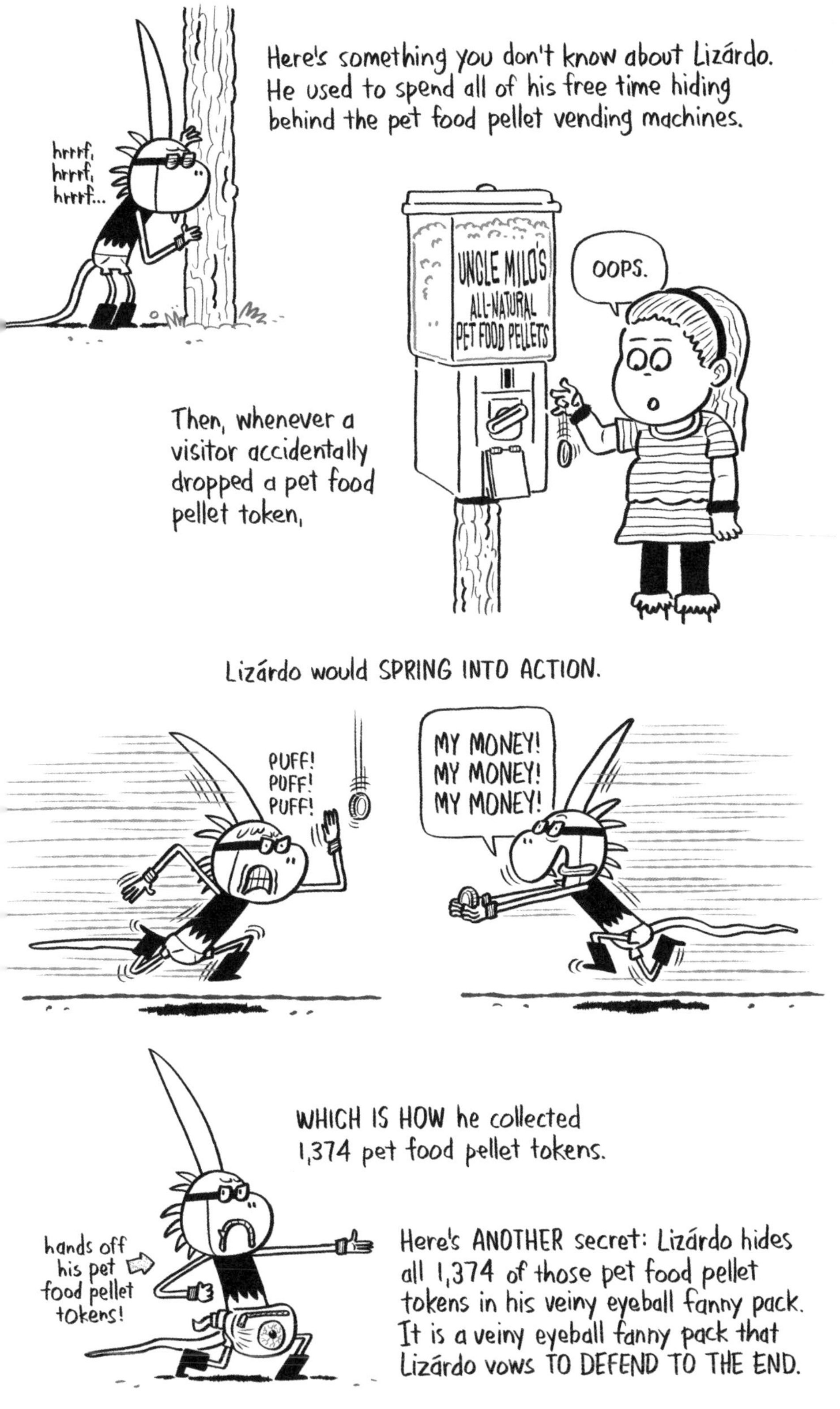
hrrrf, hrrrf, hrrrf...
Here's something you don't know about Lizárdo. He used to spend all of his free time hiding behind the pet food pellet vending machines.
UNCLE MILO'S ALL-NATURAL PET FOOD PELLETS
OOPS.
Then, whenever a visitor accidentally dropped a pet food pellet token,
Lizárdo would SPRING INTO ACTION.
PUFF! PUFF! PUFF!
MY MONEY! MY MONEY! MY MONEY!
WHICH IS HOW he collected 1,374 pet food pellet tokens.
hands off his pet food pellet tokens!
Here's ANOTHER secret: Lizárdo hides all 1,374 of those pet food pellet tokens in his veiny eyeball fanny pack. It is a veiny eyeball fanny pack that Lizárdo vows TO DEFEND TO THE END.

OUR DESTINY TO DESTINY

HEY, LOOK. This is me and my best friend Lizárdo after we escaped from that petting zoo who is DEFINITELY NOT the boss of us. Their crazy maintenance man tried to stop us, but we OUTSMARTED him.

AND SO — this is me and my best friend Lizárdo riding Tiger and Stardust to OUR DESTINY.

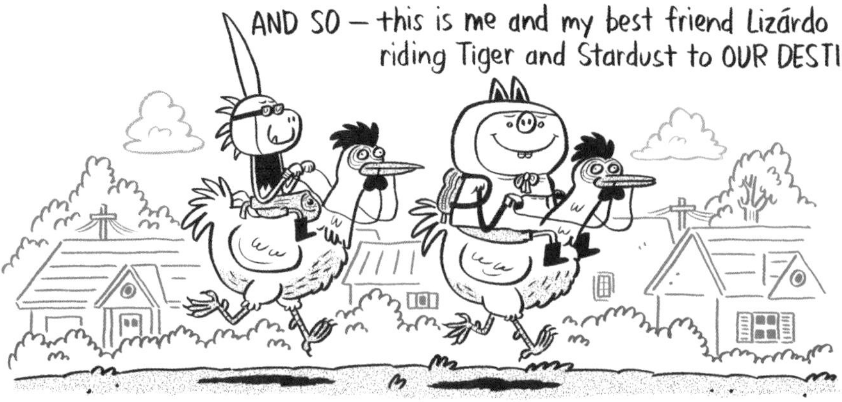

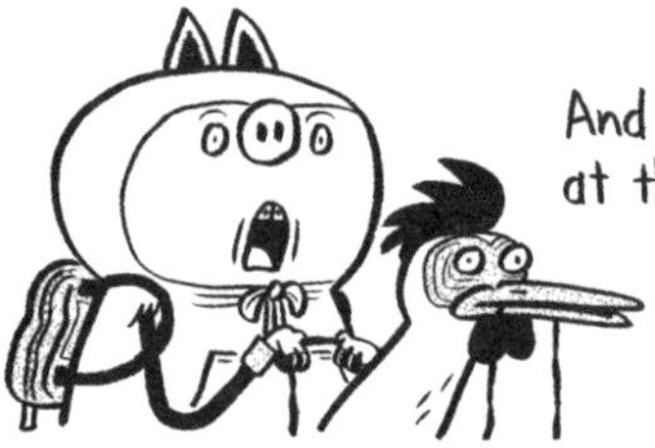

And this is me seeing OUR DESTINY — at the corner of Walnut and Pine.

Our DESTINY is a CHIHUAHUA — who is wearing a HAT — and a DIAPER — while being pushed in a BABY CARRIAGE — by a man with a FANCY MUSTACHE.

Destiny's a funny thing, Destiny is.

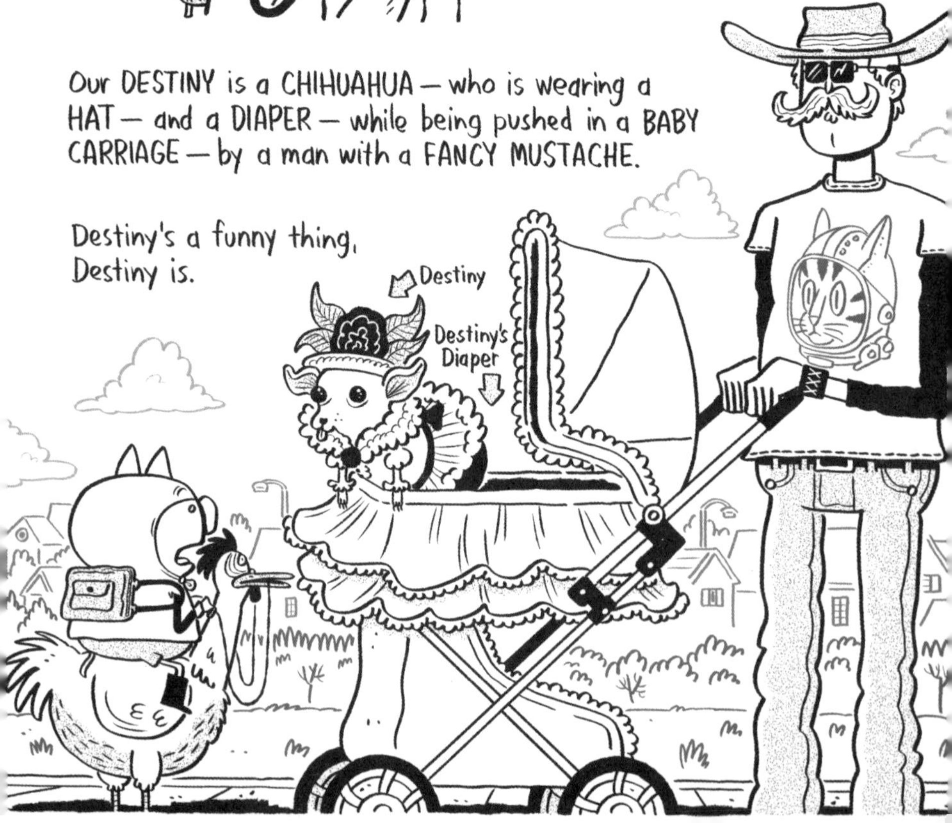
Destiny
Destiny's Diaper

"Pardon me, Your Highness," I said to the Chihuahua. "But how does a doggy like yourself become so powerful that you don't have to walk with your legs or excuse yourself to make a potty?"

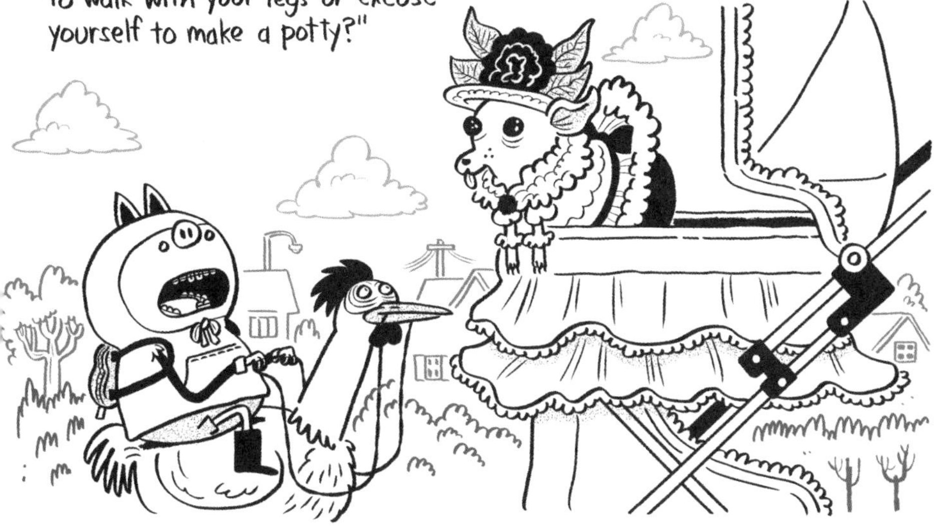

DROOL...

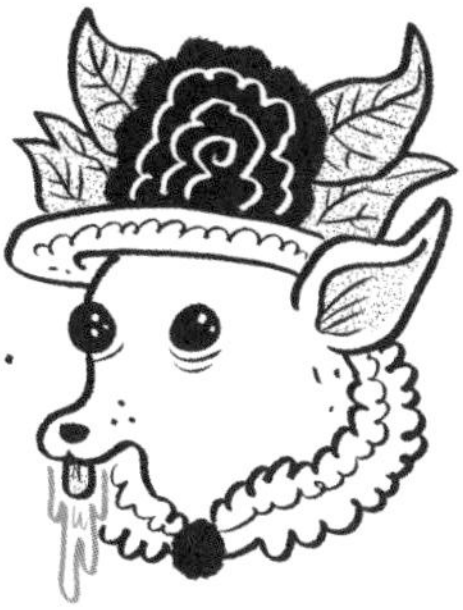

said the very powerful Chihuahua.

"Lizárdo! That Chihuahua has GOT IT MADE!" I said. "It's high time WE got in on some of those SWEET PET PERKS!"

"Yeah-yeah!" Lizárdo said. "SWEET-PET-PERKS! SWEET-PET-PERKS!"

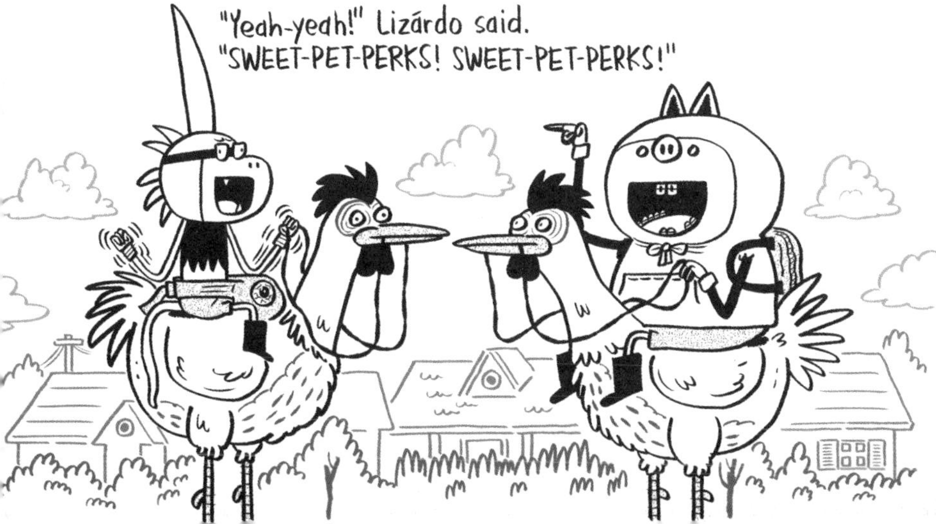

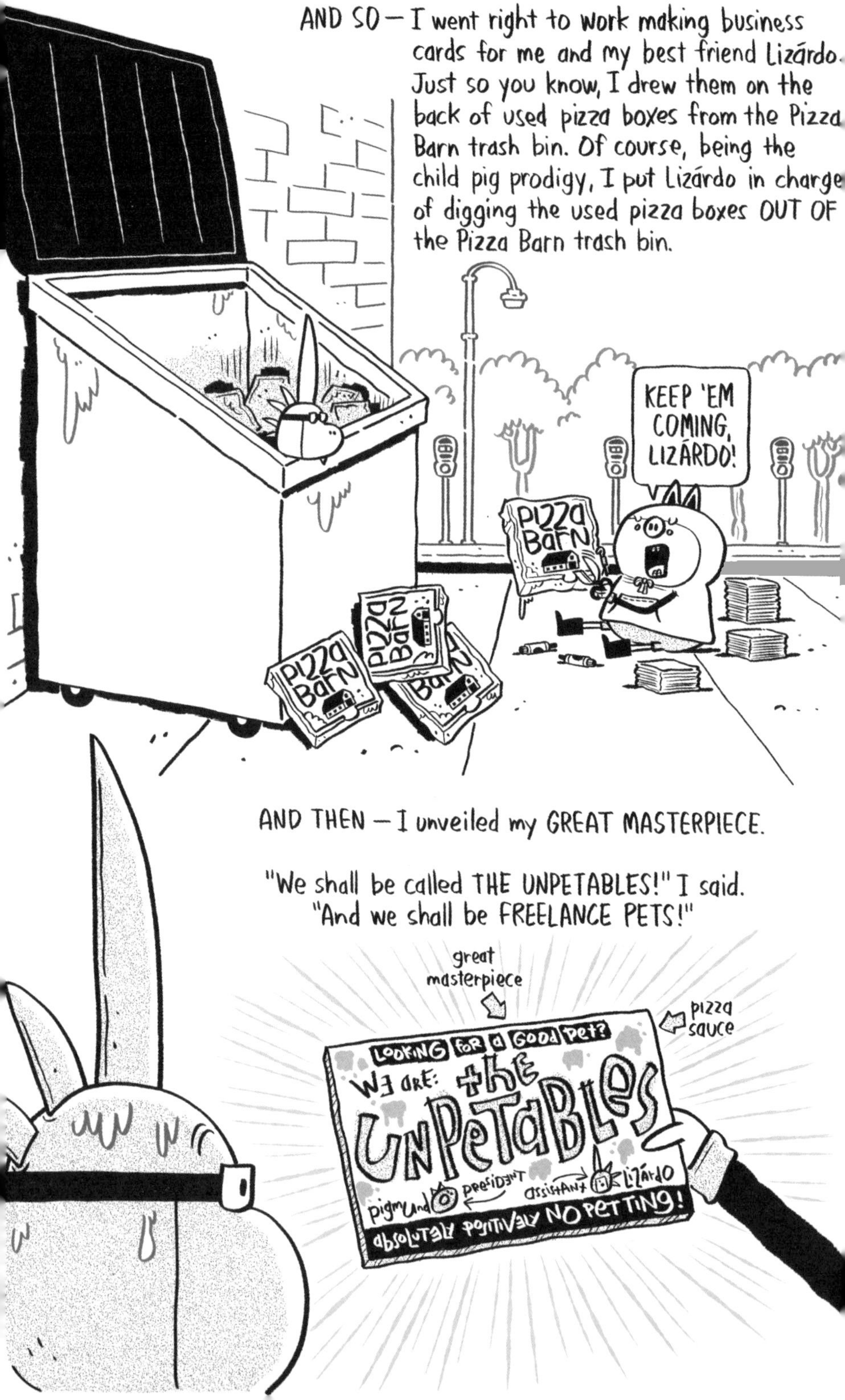
AND SO — I went right to work making business cards for me and my best friend Lizárdo. Just so you know, I drew them on the back of used pizza boxes from the Pizza Barn trash bin. Of course, being the child pig prodigy, I put Lizárdo in charge of digging the used pizza boxes OUT OF the Pizza Barn trash bin.
KEEP 'EM COMING, LIZÁRDO!
PIZZA BARN
AND THEN — I unveiled my GREAT MASTERPIECE.
"We shall be called THE UNPETABLES!" I said. "And we shall be FREELANCE PETS!"
great masterpiece
pizza sauce
LOOKING FOR A GOOD PET?
WE ARE: THE UNPETABLES
PIGMUND PRESIDENT
ASSISTANT LIZÁRDO
ABSOLUTELY POSITIVELY NO PETTING!

But Lizárdo didn't GET IT.
"What-be-a-freelance-pet?"
he asked.

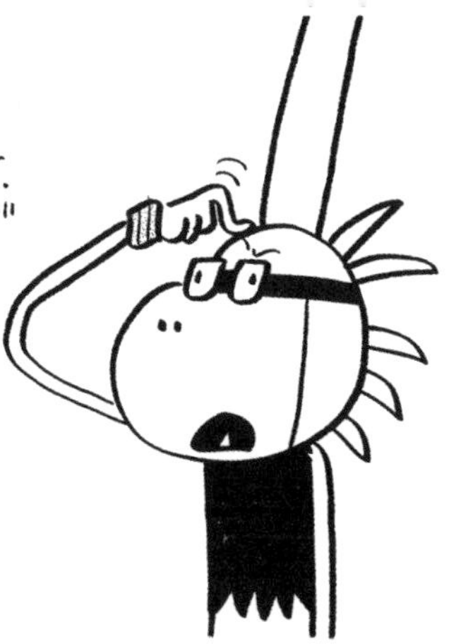

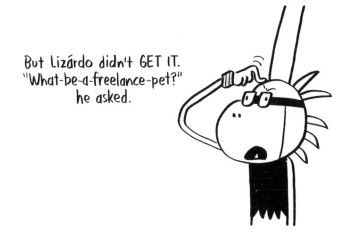

"Lemme explain. A FREELANCE PET is like a regular pet — who can walk away from their dumb pet job ANY TIME THEY WANT."

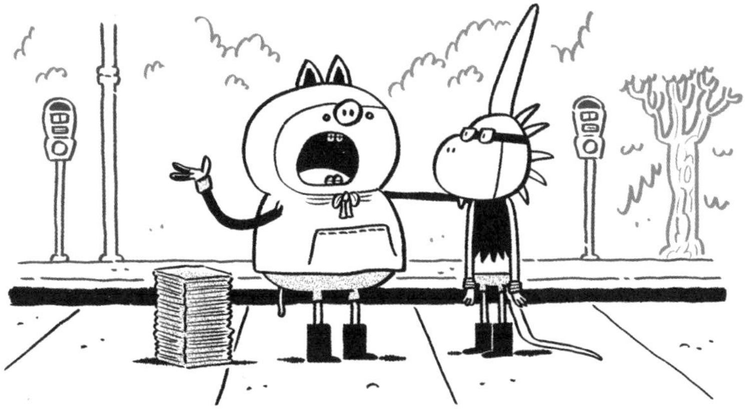

I won't lie. Sometimes the hardest part about being a child pig prodigy is explaining things to people who are NOT child pig prodigies.

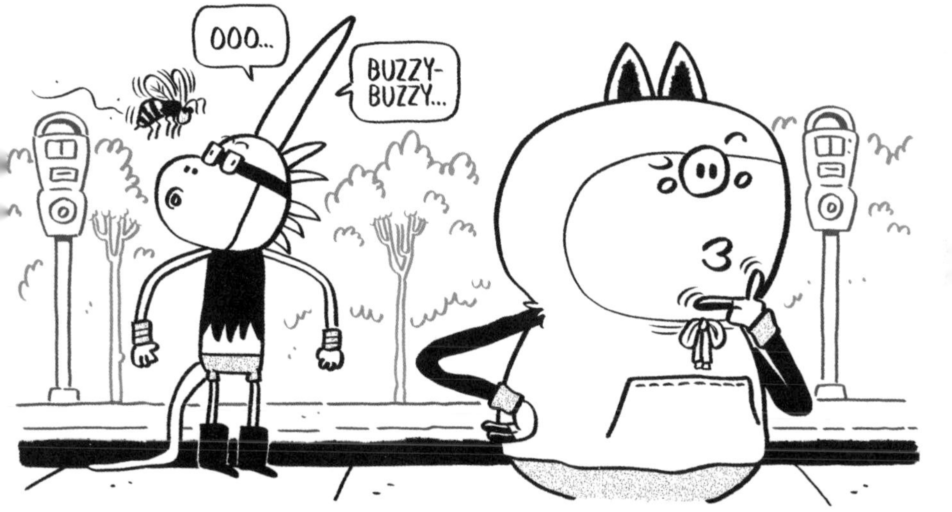
OOO...
BUZZY-
BUZZY...

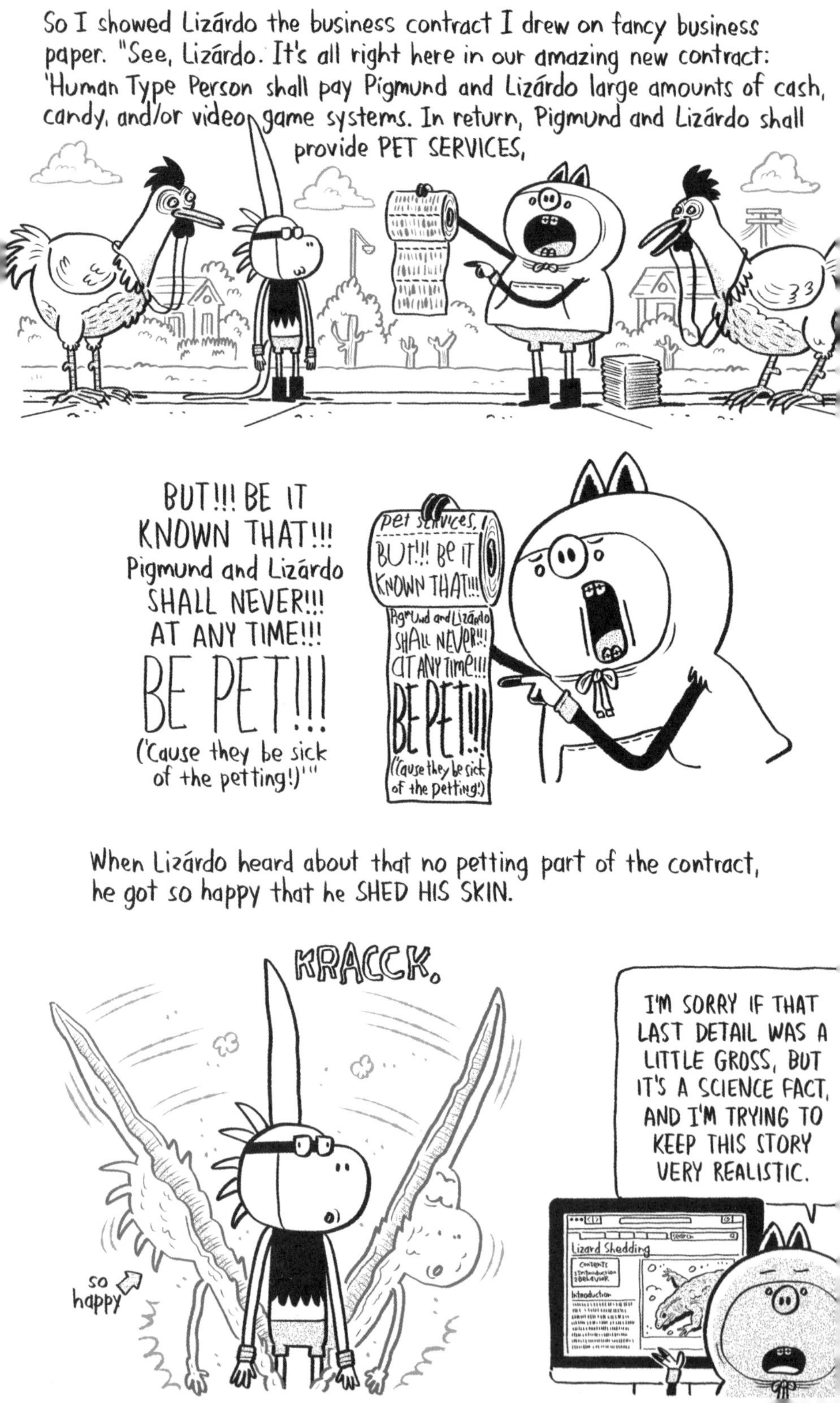

So I showed Lizárdo the business contract I drew on fancy business paper. "See, Lizárdo. It's all right here in our amazing new contract: 'Human Type Person shall pay Pigmund and Lizárdo large amounts of cash, candy, and/or video game systems. In return, Pigmund and Lizárdo shall provide PET SERVICES,
BUT!!! BE IT KNOWN THAT!!! Pigmund and Lizárdo SHALL NEVER!!! AT ANY TIME!!! BE PET!!! ('Cause they be sick of the petting!)'"
pet services, BUT!!! BE IT KNOWN THAT!!! Pigmund and Lizárdo SHALL NEVER!!! AT ANY TIME!!! BE PET!!! ('cause they be sick of the petting!)
When Lizárdo heard about that no petting part of the contract, he got so happy that he SHED HIS SKIN.
KRACCK.
so happy
I'M SORRY IF THAT LAST DETAIL WAS A LITTLE GROSS, BUT IT'S A SCIENCE FACT, AND I'M TRYING TO KEEP THIS STORY VERY REALISTIC.
Lizard Shedding
Contents
Introduction

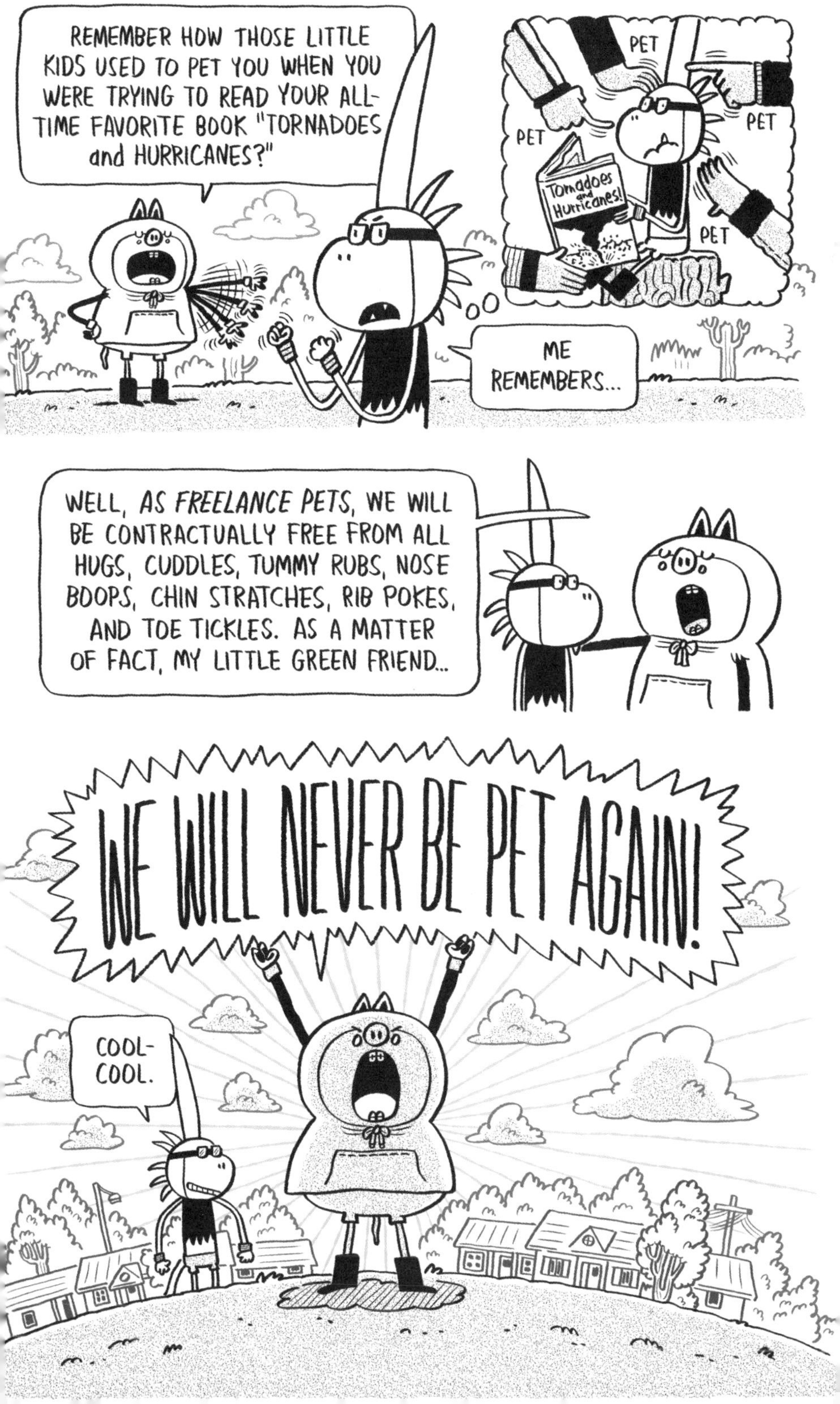

REMEMBER HOW THOSE LITTLE KIDS USED TO PET YOU WHEN YOU WERE TRYING TO READ YOUR ALL-TIME FAVORITE BOOK "TORNADOES and HURRICANES?"
PET
PET
PET
PET
Tornadoes and Hurricanes!
ME REMEMBERS...
WELL, AS FREELANCE PETS, WE WILL BE CONTRACTUALLY FREE FROM ALL HUGS, CUDDLES, TUMMY RUBS, NOSE BOOPS, CHIN STRATCHES, RIB POKES, AND TOE TICKLES. AS A MATTER OF FACT, MY LITTLE GREEN FRIEND...
WE WILL NEVER BE PET AGAIN!
COOL-COOL.

Adventure 3

greetings from
HOMETOWN

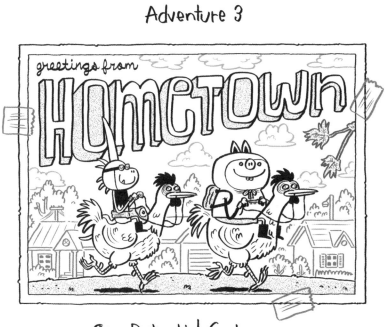

Our Potential Customers

POTENTIAL CUSTOMER #1

THE UNPETABLES freelance pet business was in business. But the first rule of business is to find some business, so we went on a Finding Business Quest.

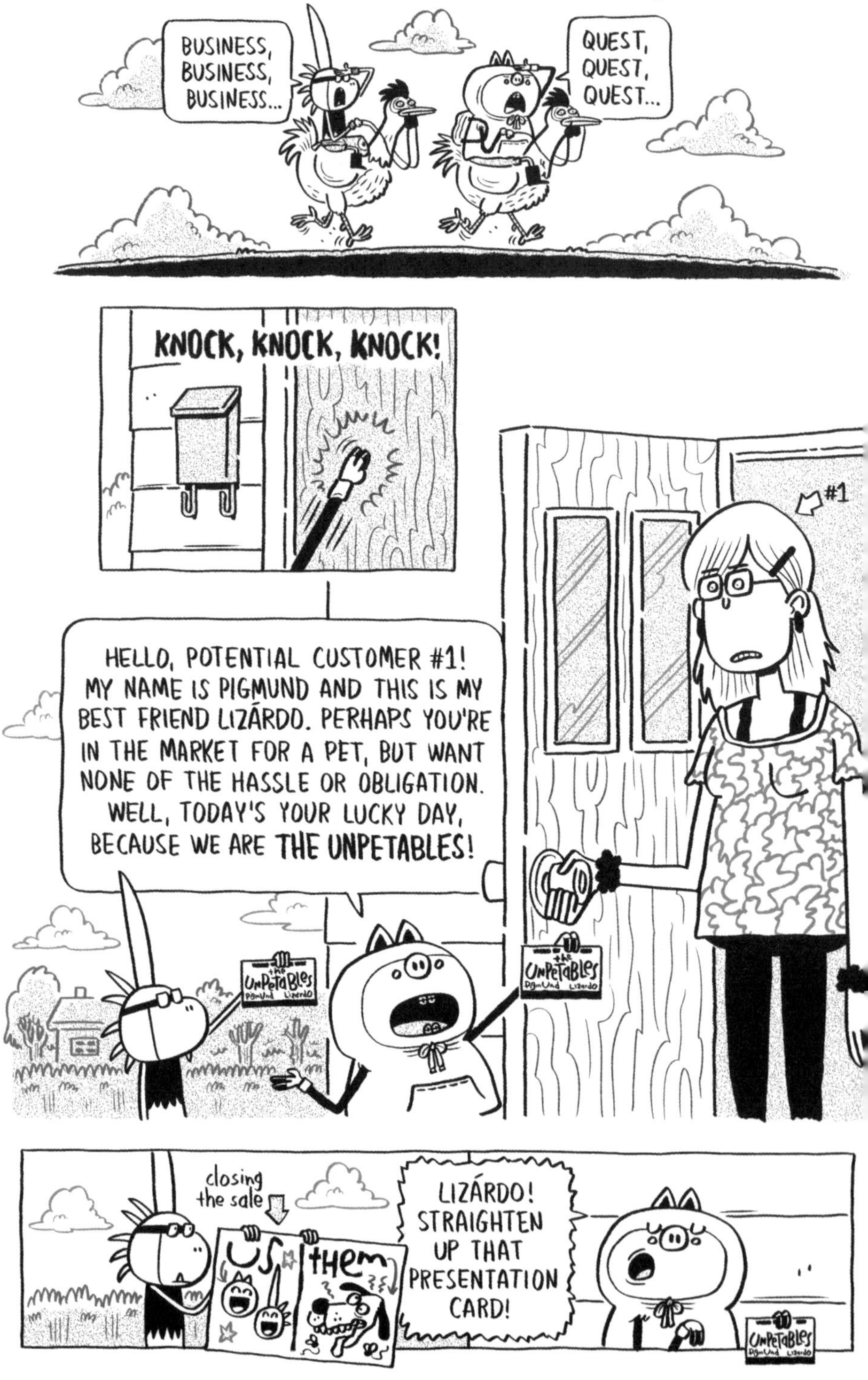
BUSINESS, BUSINESS, BUSINESS...
QUEST, QUEST, QUEST...
KNOCK, KNOCK, KNOCK!
#1
HELLO, POTENTIAL CUSTOMER #1! MY NAME IS PIGMUND AND THIS IS MY BEST FRIEND LIZÁRDO. PERHAPS YOU'RE IN THE MARKET FOR A PET, BUT WANT NONE OF THE HASSLE OR OBLIGATION. WELL, TODAY'S YOUR LUCKY DAY, BECAUSE WE ARE THE UNPETABLES!
the UNPETABLES
closing the sale
US
them
LIZÁRDO! STRAIGHTEN UP THAT PRESENTATION CARD!

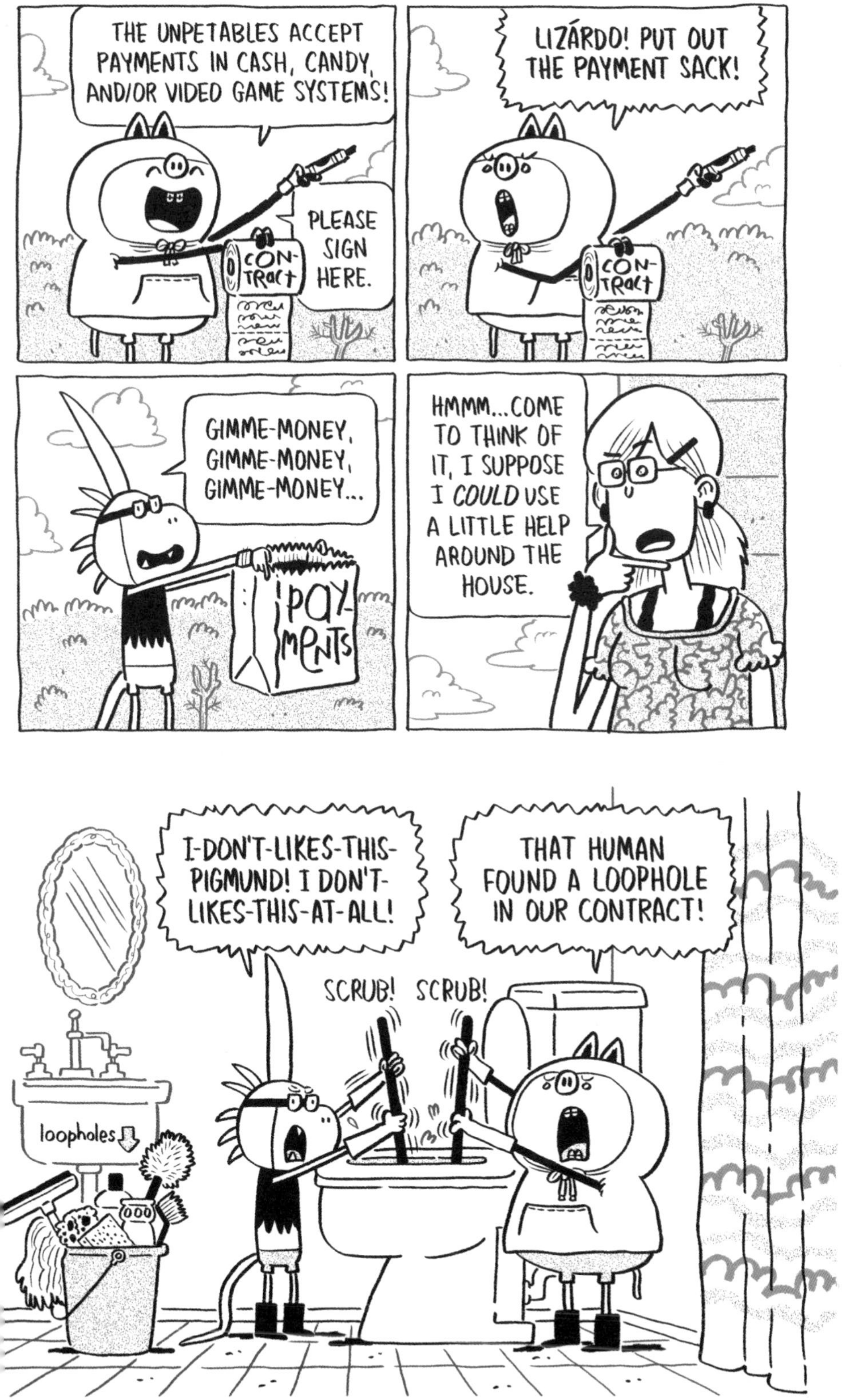
THE UNPETABLES ACCEPT PAYMENTS IN CASH, CANDY, AND/OR VIDEO GAME SYSTEMS!
PLEASE SIGN HERE.
CONTRACT
LIZÁRDO! PUT OUT THE PAYMENT SACK!
CONTRACT
GIMME-MONEY, GIMME-MONEY, GIMME-MONEY...
PAYMENTS
HMMM...COME TO THINK OF IT, I SUPPOSE I *COULD* USE A LITTLE HELP AROUND THE HOUSE.
I-DON'T-LIKES-THIS-PIGMUND! I DON'T-LIKES-THIS-AT-ALL!
THAT HUMAN FOUND A LOOPHOLE IN OUR CONTRACT!
SCRUB! SCRUB!
loopholes

POTENTIAL CUSTOMER #3

"Lemme explain it this way," I explained to Potential Customer #3.

"Dogs are too dirty, and cats are too clean, and birds—well, birds are related to Velociraptors, and who can sleep at night with those crazy psychos living under your roof?"

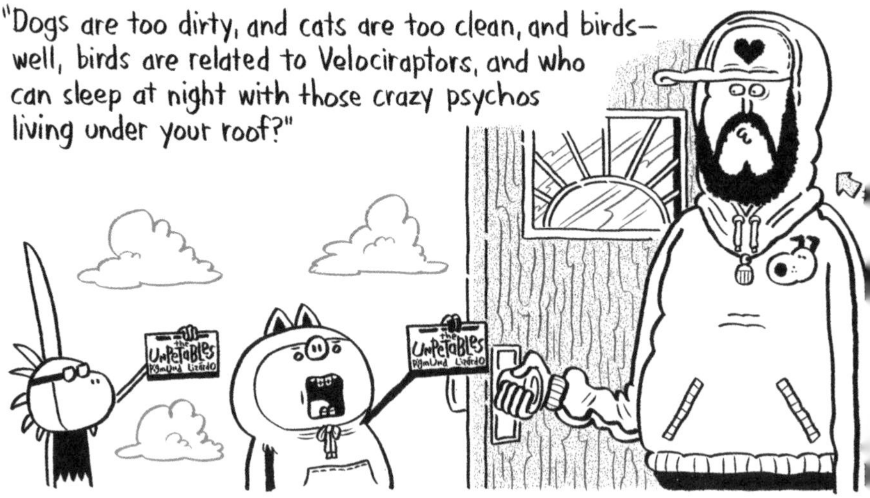

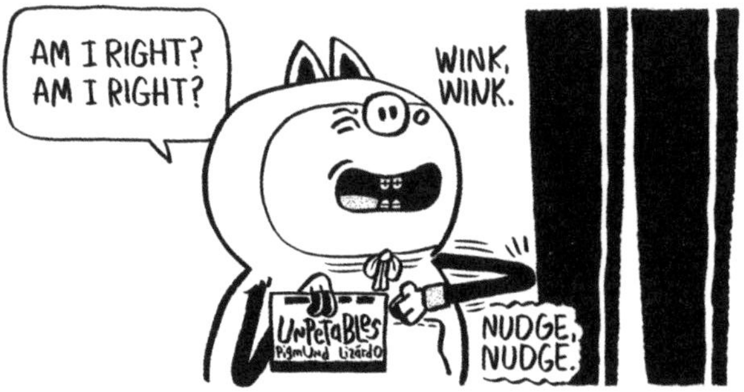
AM I RIGHT? AM I RIGHT?
WINK, WINK.
NUDGE, NUDGE.

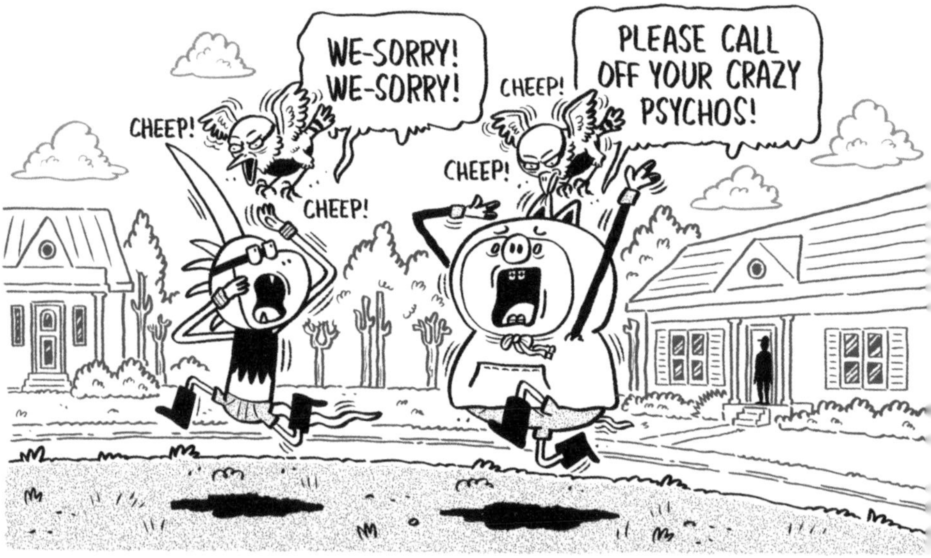
WE-SORRY! WE-SORRY!
CHEEP!
PLEASE CALL OFF YOUR CRAZY PSYCHOS!
CHEEP!
CHEEP!
CHEEP!

POTENTIAL CUSTOMER #7

"Good afternoon!" I said to Potential Customer #7. "We have located and returned your lost cat. Now pay us BIG CASH MONEY."

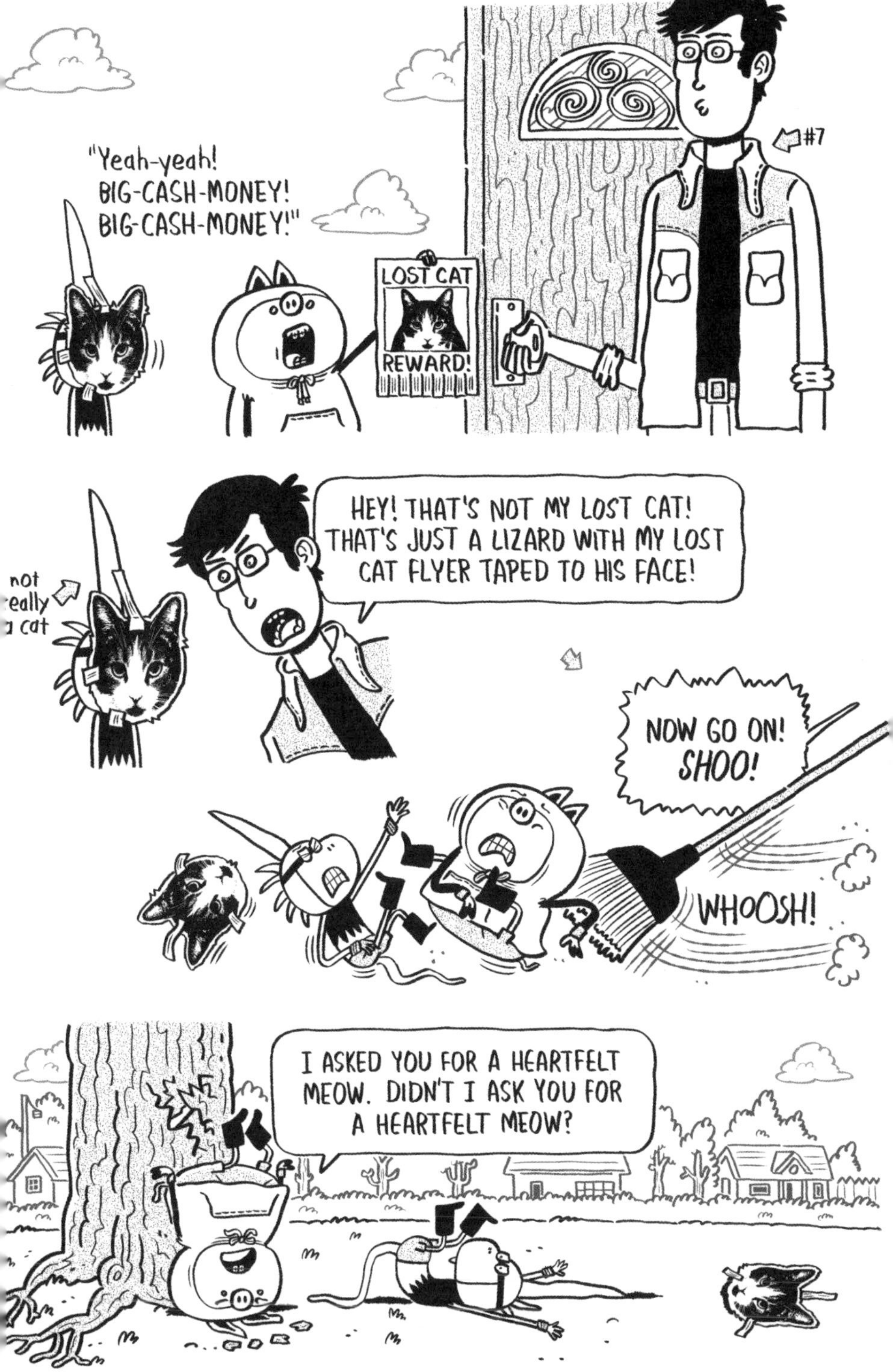
"Yeah-yeah!
BIG-CASH-MONEY!
BIG-CASH-MONEY!"
LOST CAT
REWARD!
#7
HEY! THAT'S NOT MY LOST CAT! THAT'S JUST A LIZARD WITH MY LOST CAT FLYER TAPED TO HIS FACE!
not
eally
cat
NOW GO ON! SHOO!
WHOOSH!
I ASKED YOU FOR A HEARTFELT MEOW. DIDN'T I ASK YOU FOR A HEARTFELT MEOW?

POTENTIAL CUSTOMER #12

"Welcome to my home," said Potential Customer #12. "I think you pets are really going to like it here!"

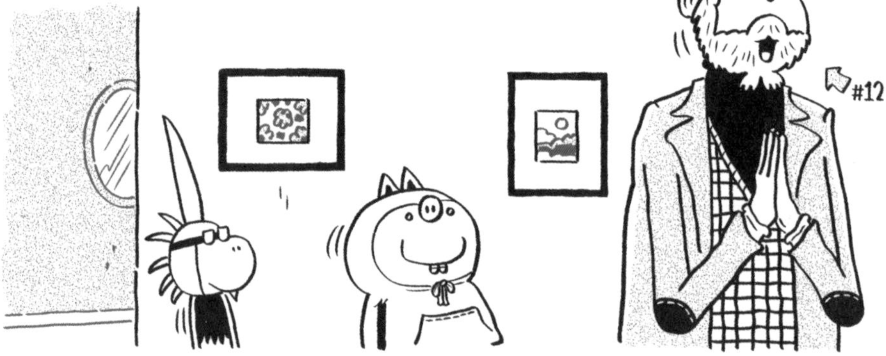
#12

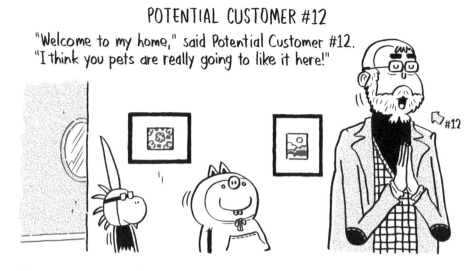

"Of course, as a substitute music teacher, I will require each of you to log in SEVEN AND ONE HALF HOURS of classical music practice every day."

"Now, tell me, do you prefer the violin, the cello, or the harp?"

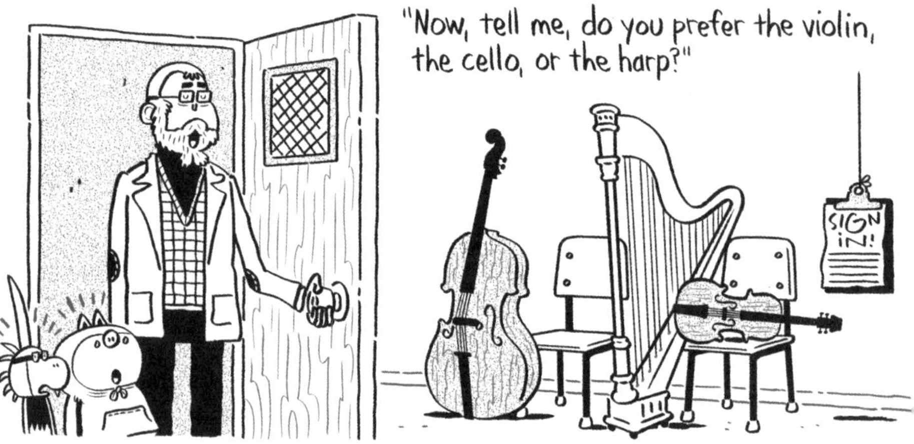
SIGN IN!

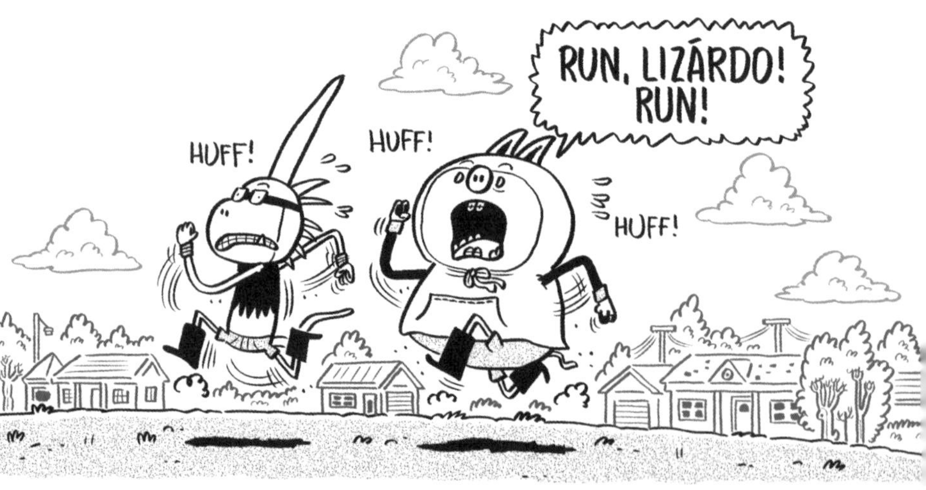
RUN, LIZÁRDO! RUN!
HUFF!
HUFF!
HUFF!

POTENTIAL CUSTOMER #19

"Well, aren't you two the most adorable pets?" said Potential Customer #19.

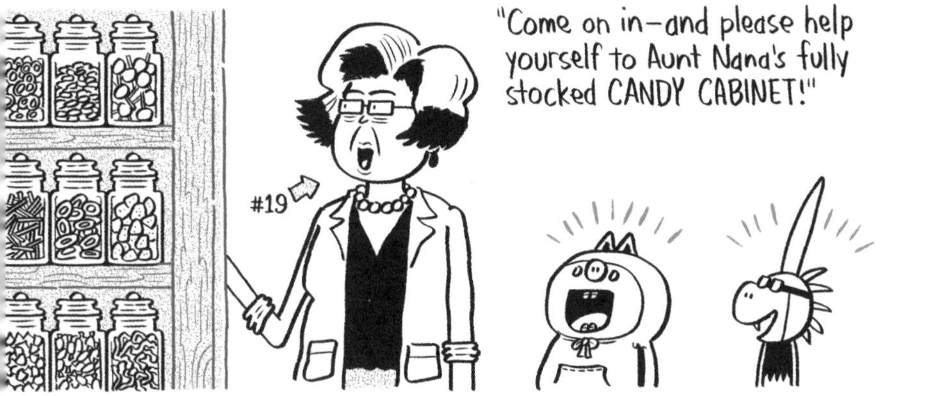
"Come on in—and please help yourself to Aunt Nana's fully stocked CANDY CABINET!"
#19

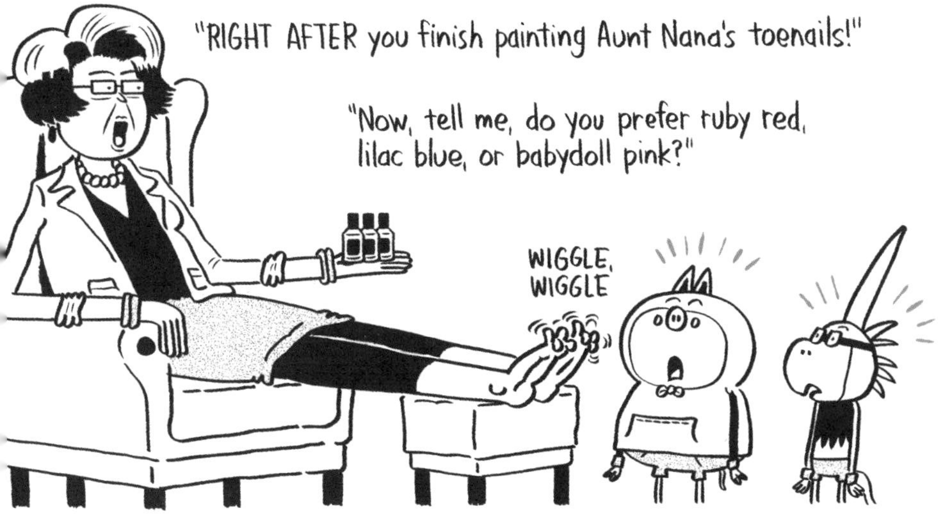
"RIGHT AFTER you finish painting Aunt Nana's toenails!"
"Now, tell me, do you prefer ruby red, lilac blue, or babydoll pink?"
WIGGLE, WIGGLE

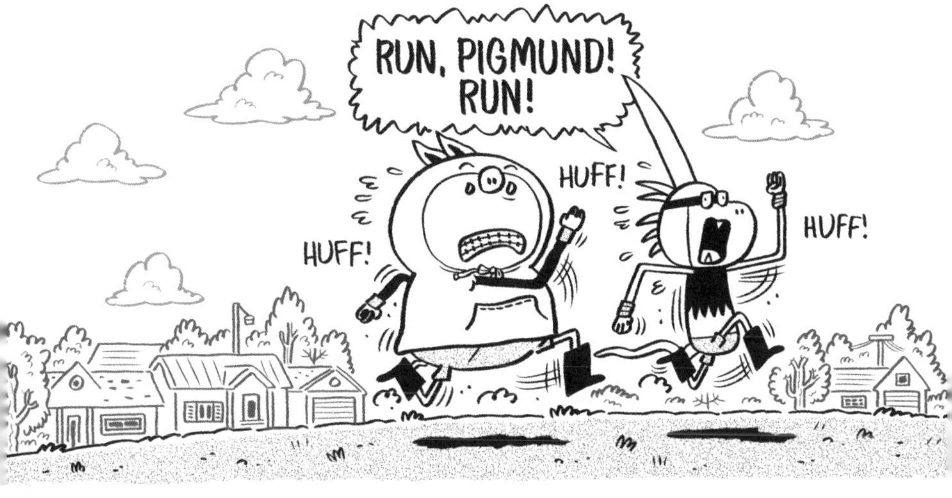
RUN, PIGMUND! RUN!
HUFF!
HUFF!
HUFF!

POTENTIAL CUSTOMER #23

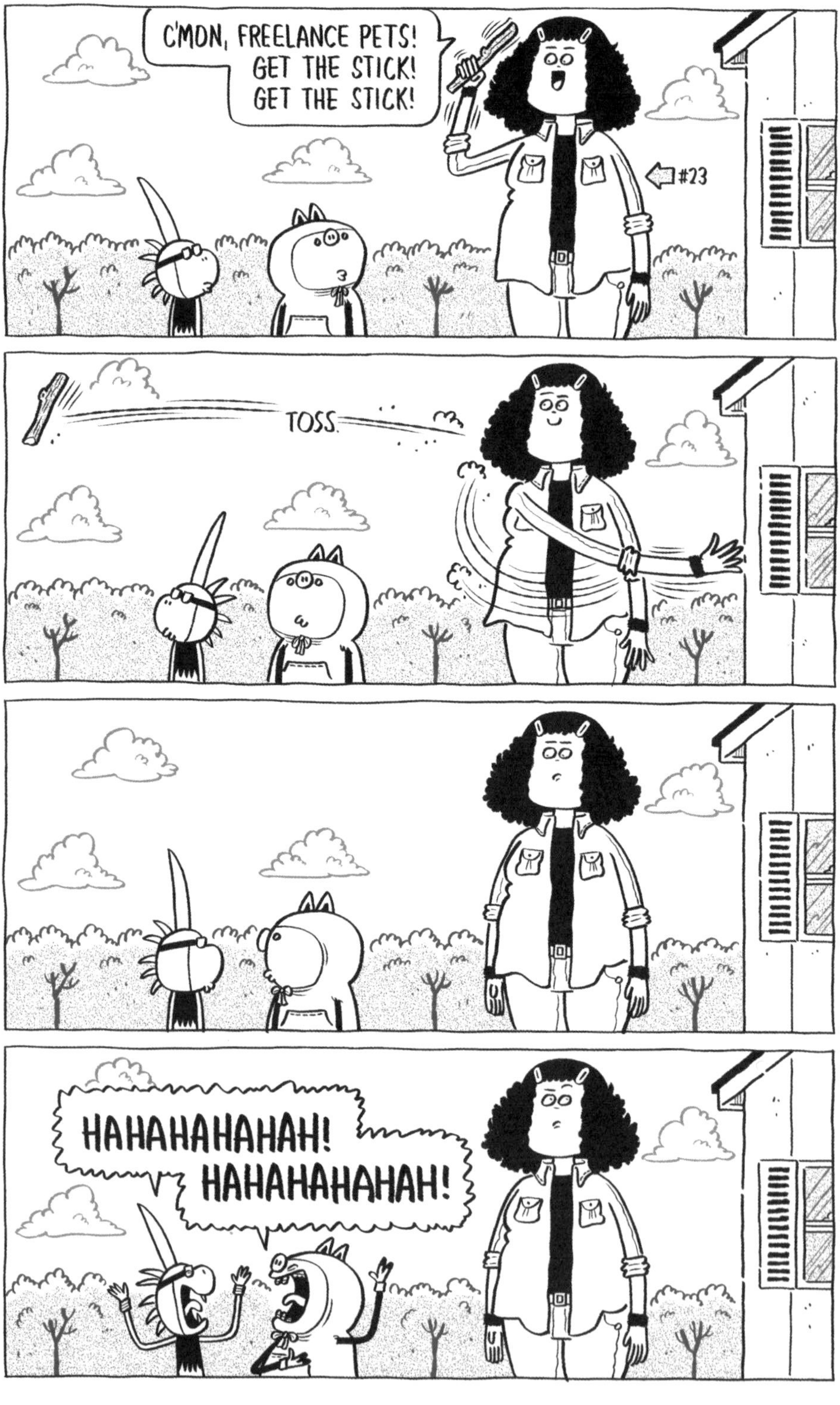
C'MON, FREELANCE PETS! GET THE STICK! GET THE STICK!
#23
TOSS
HAHAHAHAHAH!
HAHAHAHAHAH!

POTENTIAL CUSTOMER #34

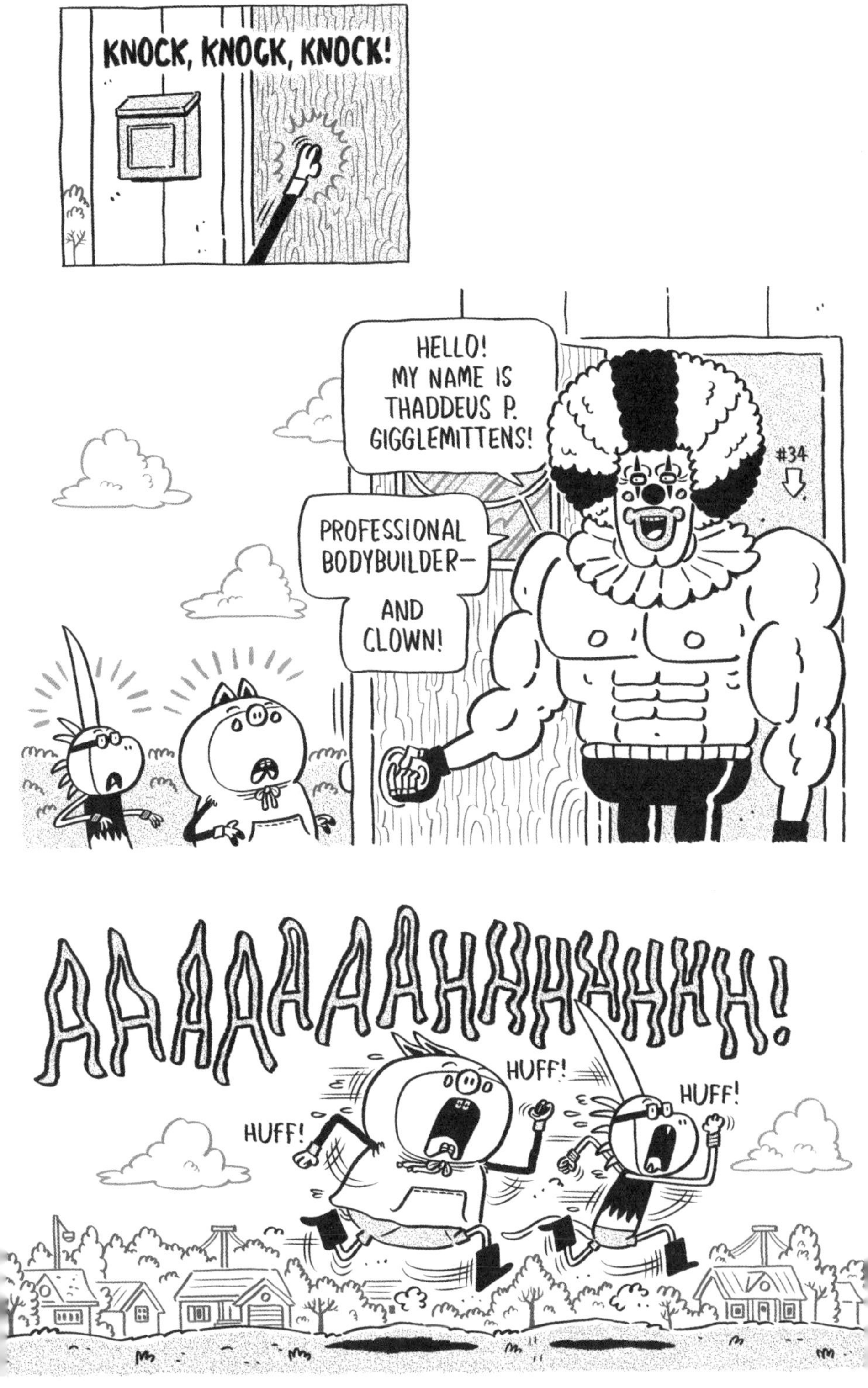

KNOCK, KNOCK, KNOCK!
HELLO! MY NAME IS THADDEUS P. GIGGLEMITTENS!
PROFESSIONAL BODYBUILDER—
AND CLOWN!
#34
AAAAAAHHHHHHH!
HUFF!
HUFF!
HUFF!

THE RETURN OF MAINTENANCE MAN KENNY

MEANWHILE – as me and Lizárdo looked for super-high-paying pet jobs – Maintenance Man Kenny was REBUILDING HIS EMPIRE.

Which he did by pulling his electric cart out of Big Fishy River,

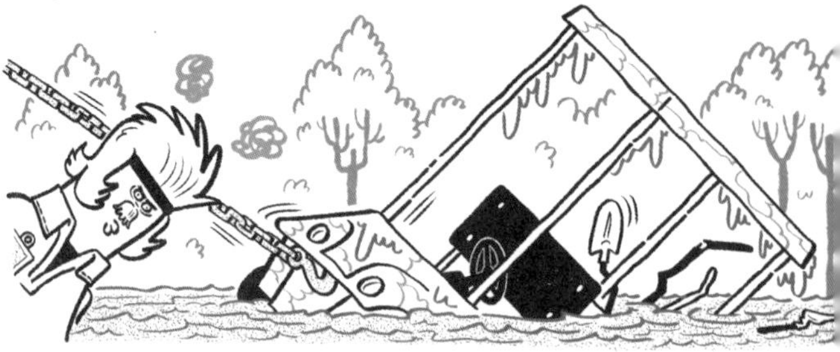

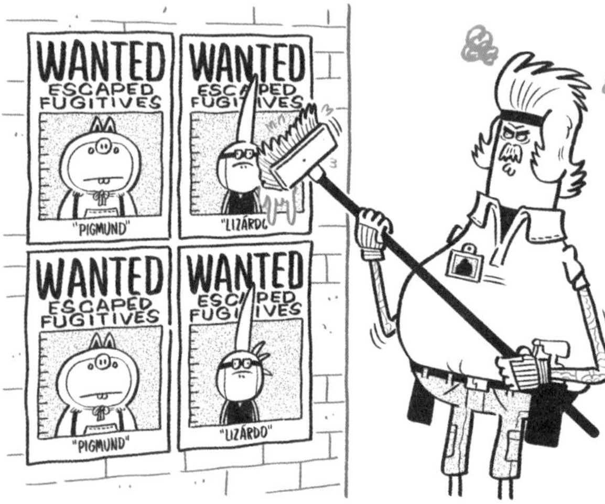
WANTED
ESCAPED FUGITIVES
"PIGMUND"
"LIZÁRDO"

posting 23 WANTED: ESCAPED FUGITIVES posters,

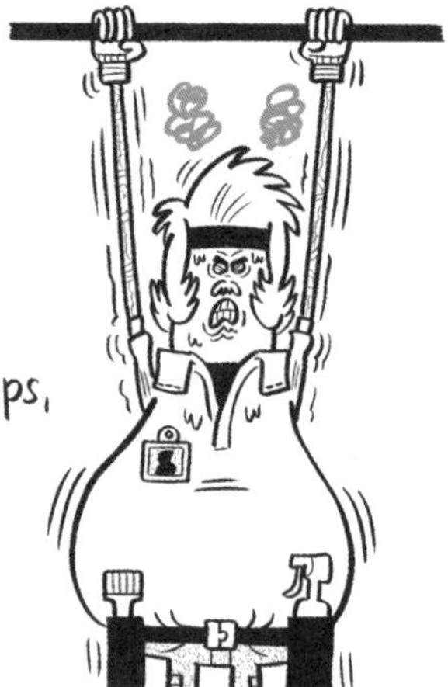

completing 6 and a half pull-ups,

and recruiting 11 fluffy bunny minions.

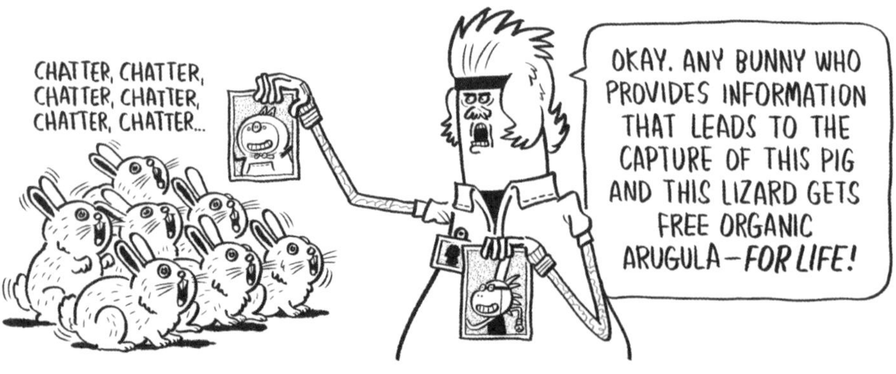
CHATTER, CHATTER, CHATTER, CHATTER, CHATTER, CHATTER...
OKAY. ANY BUNNY WHO PROVIDES INFORMATION THAT LEADS TO THE CAPTURE OF THIS PIG AND THIS LIZARD GETS FREE ORGANIC ARUGULA—*FOR LIFE!*

AND SO—
if you visit our hometown of Hometown, you may see an angry maintenance man and his team of fluffy bunny suck-ups. Do NOT be alarmed. They're just searching for me and my best friend Lizárdo.

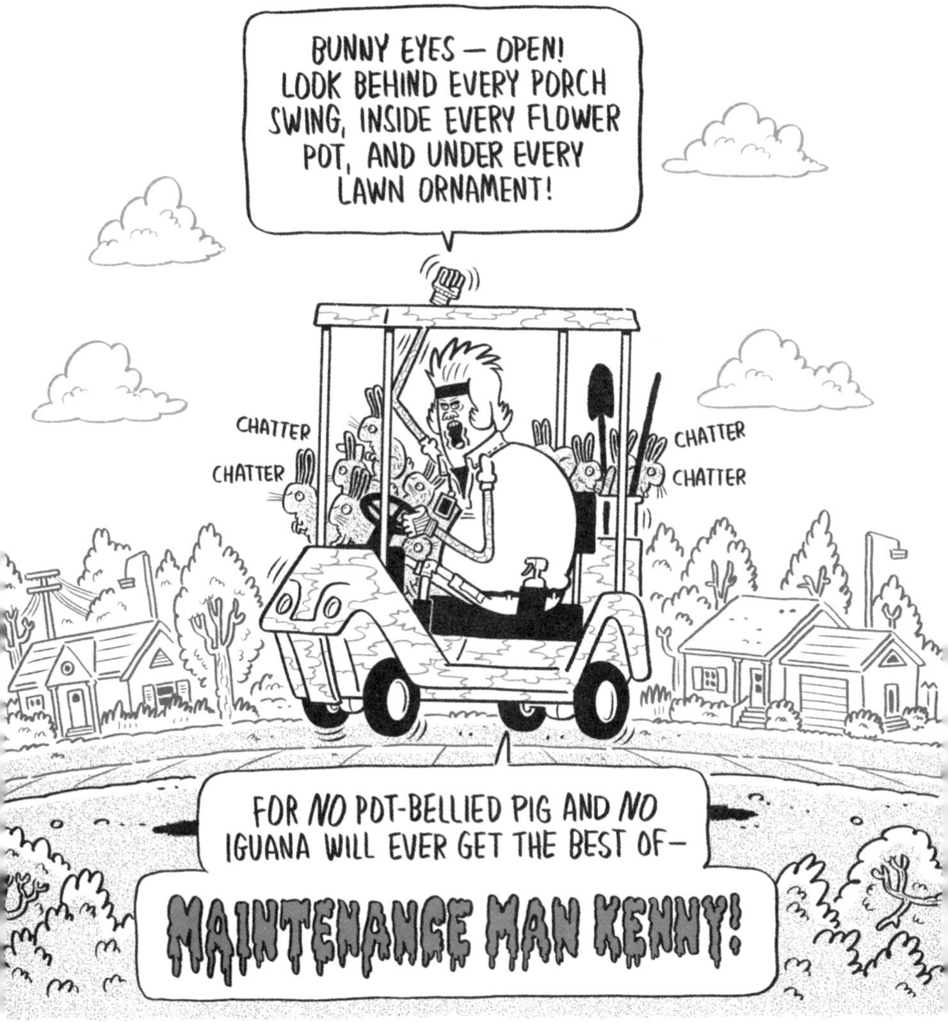
BUNNY EYES — OPEN! LOOK BEHIND EVERY PORCH SWING, INSIDE EVERY FLOWER POT, AND UNDER EVERY LAWN ORNAMENT!
CHATTER
CHATTER
CHATTER
CHATTER
FOR *NO* POT-BELLIED PIG AND *NO* IGUANA WILL EVER GET THE BEST OF—
MAINTENANCE MAN KENNY!

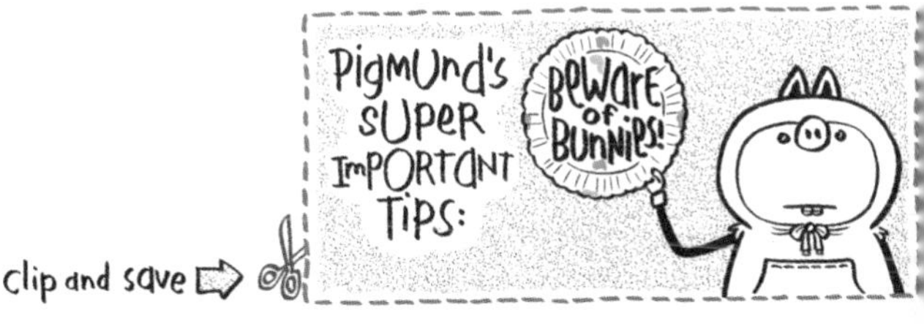
Clip and save
PigmUnd's SUPER IMPORTANT TIPS:
Beware of Bunnies!

Adventure 4

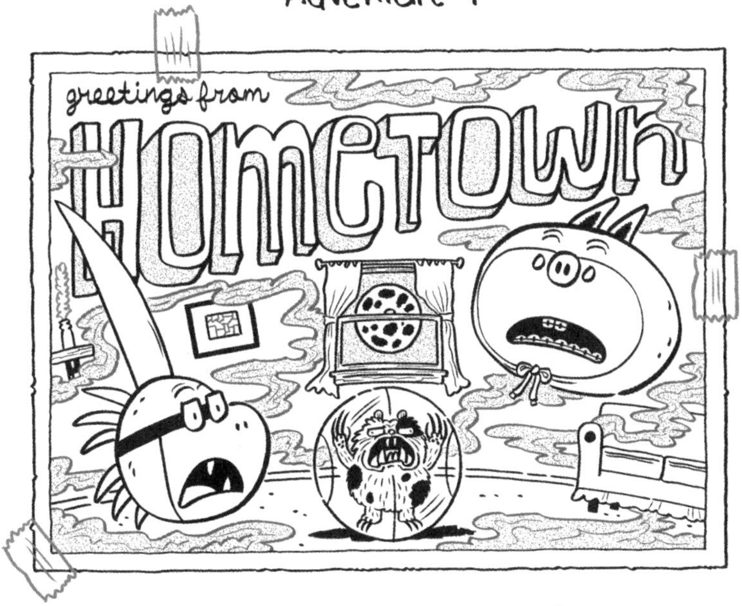
greetings from
HOMETOWN

Curse Of the Were-pets

POTENTIAL CUSTOMER # 74

Once upon a time, a wise person drew an inspirational poster on the front of a used pizza box. And I should know. That wise person was ME.

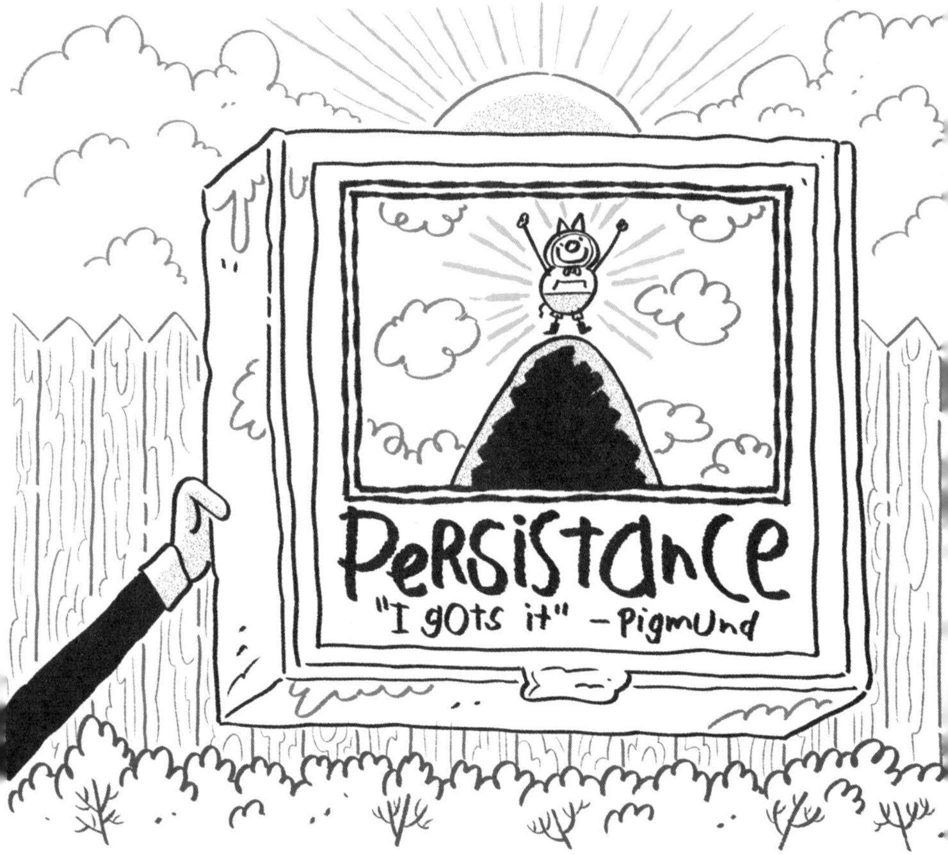
PeRSISTance
"I gOts it" -PigmUnd

And my inspirational poster was right. Because on our 74th try for a Potential Customer, The Unpetables struck GOLD. And that gold's name was CHAD.

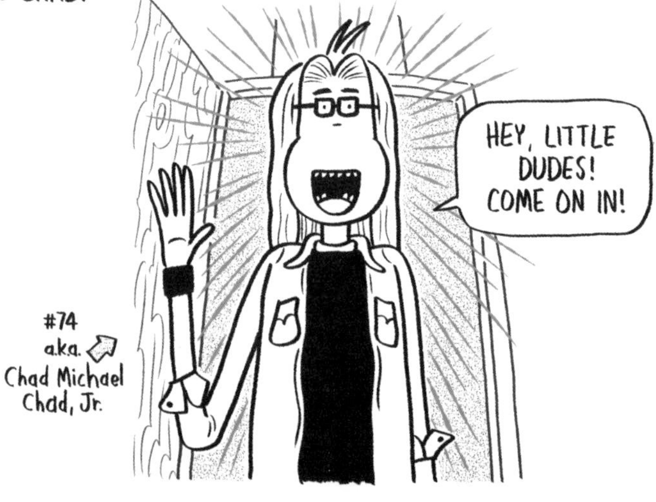
HEY, LITTLE DUDES! COME ON IN!
#74 a.k.a. Chad Michael Chad, Jr.

Chad lives in an apartment filled with great and valuable treasures. Great and valuable treasures like comic books, toys, manga, anime, trading cards, plastic models, and collectible action figures.

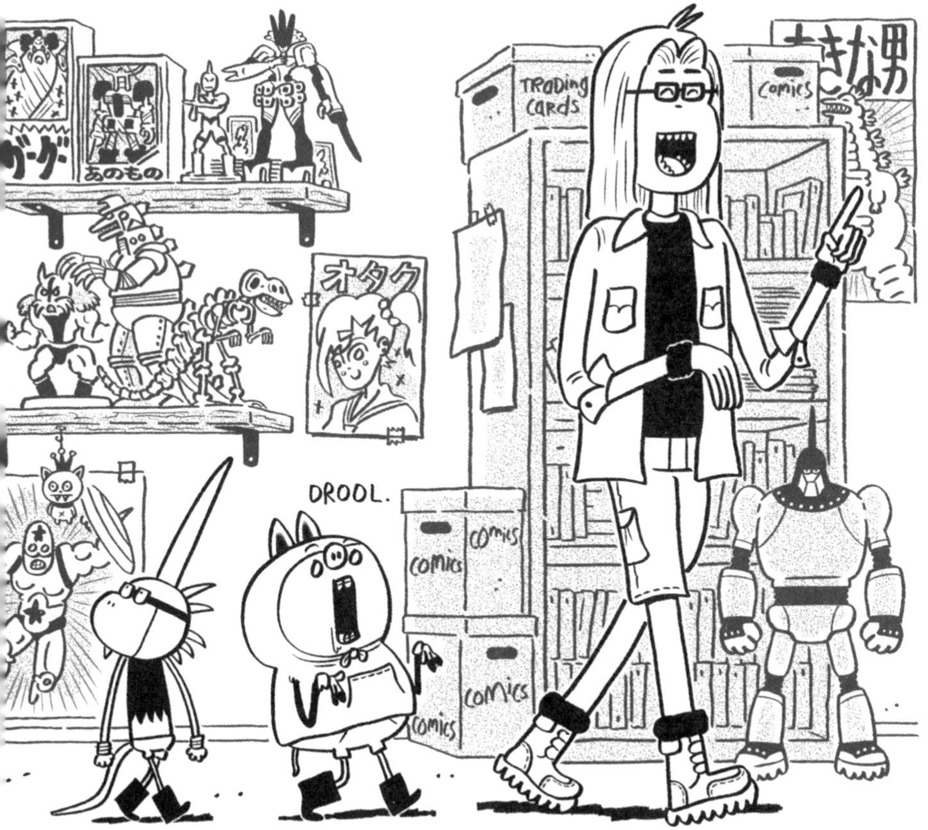
TRADING CARDS
COMICS
オタク
DROOL.
COMICS
COMICS
COMICS
COMICS

It is, without a doubt, the single greatest apartment on the face of the living earth.

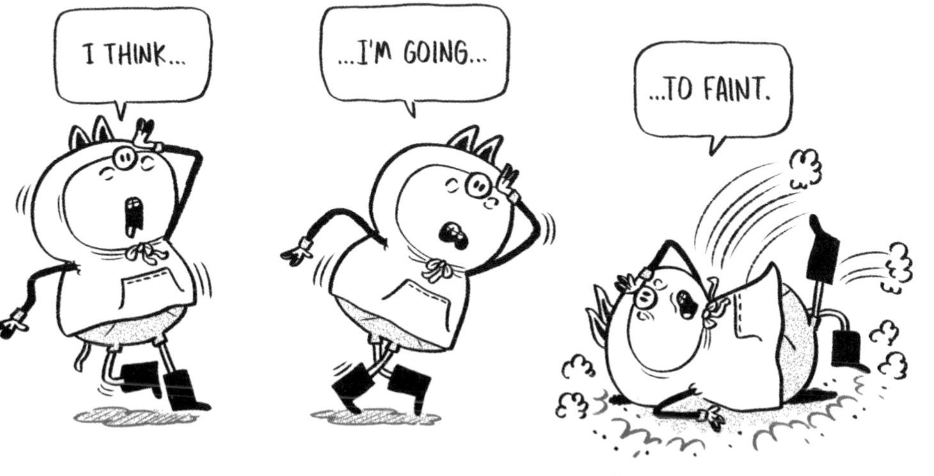
I THINK...
...I'M GOING...
...TO FAINT.

But, as always, Lizárdo doesn't GET IT.

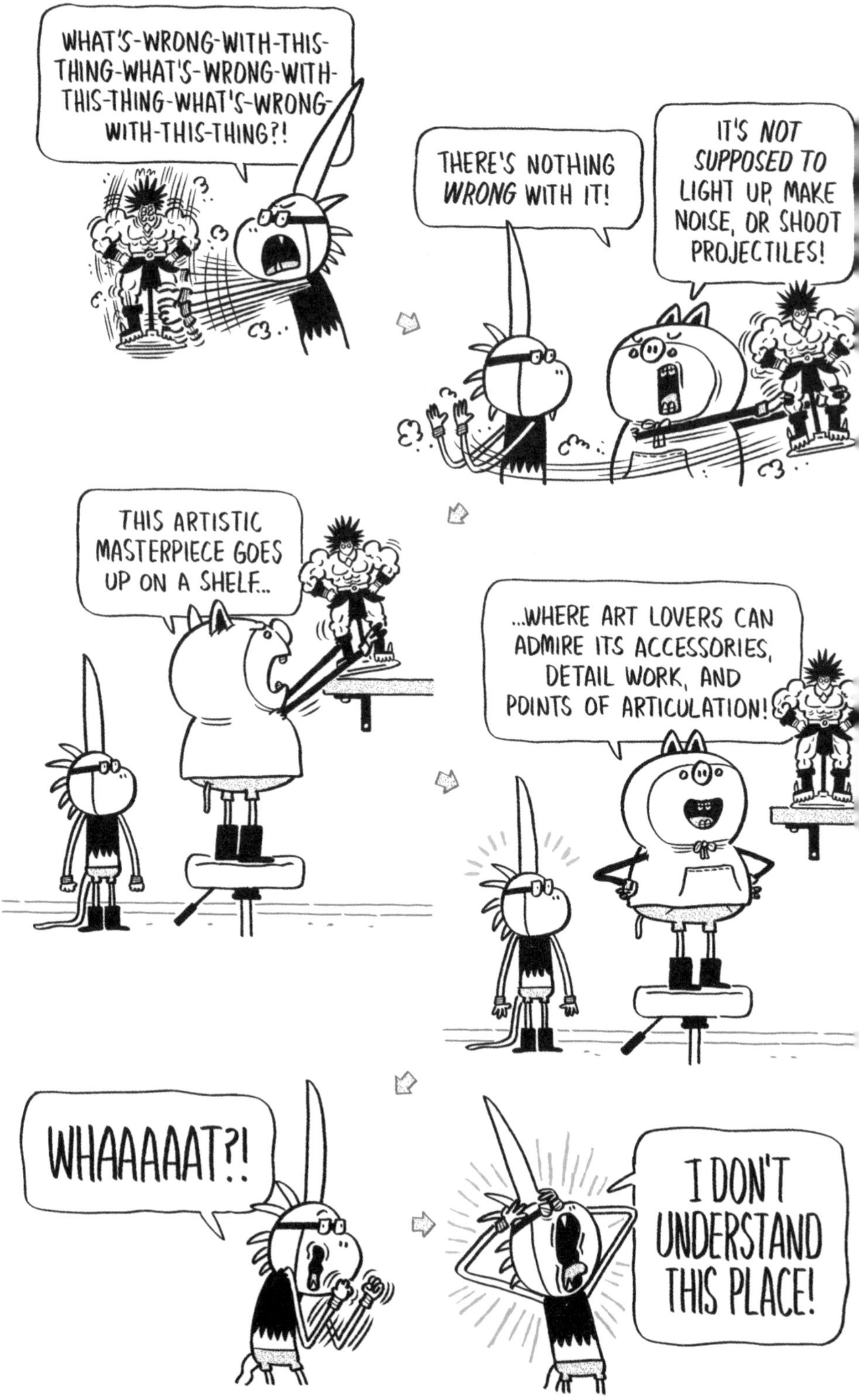
WHAT'S-WRONG-WITH-THIS-THING-WHAT'S-WRONG-WITH-THIS-THING-WHAT'S-WRONG-WITH-THIS-THING?!
THERE'S NOTHING *WRONG* WITH IT!
IT'S *NOT SUPPOSED* TO LIGHT UP, MAKE NOISE, OR SHOOT PROJECTILES!
THIS ARTISTIC MASTERPIECE GOES UP ON A SHELF...
...WHERE ART LOVERS CAN ADMIRE ITS ACCESSORIES, DETAIL WORK, AND POINTS OF ARTICULATION!
WHAAAAAT?!
I DON'T UNDERSTAND THIS PLACE!

No. Lizárdo is NOT a fan of artistic masterpieces.

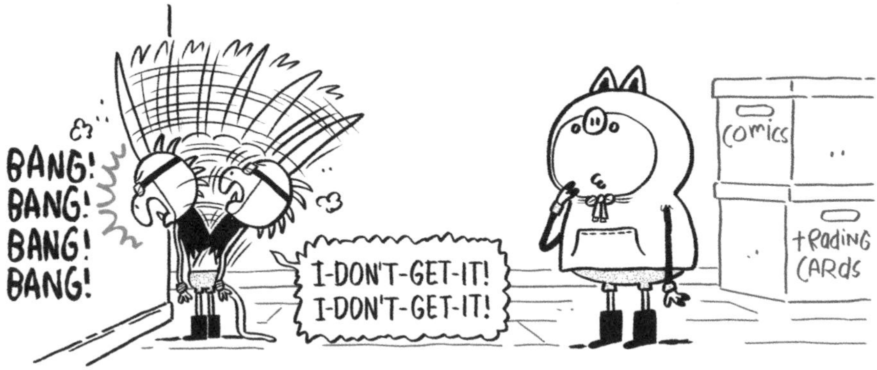
BANG! BANG! BANG! BANG!
I-DON'T-GET-IT! I-DON'T-GET-IT!
COMICS
TRADING CARDS

But then, super problem solver Chad gave Lizárdo a toy that would CHANGE HIS LIFE FOREVER.

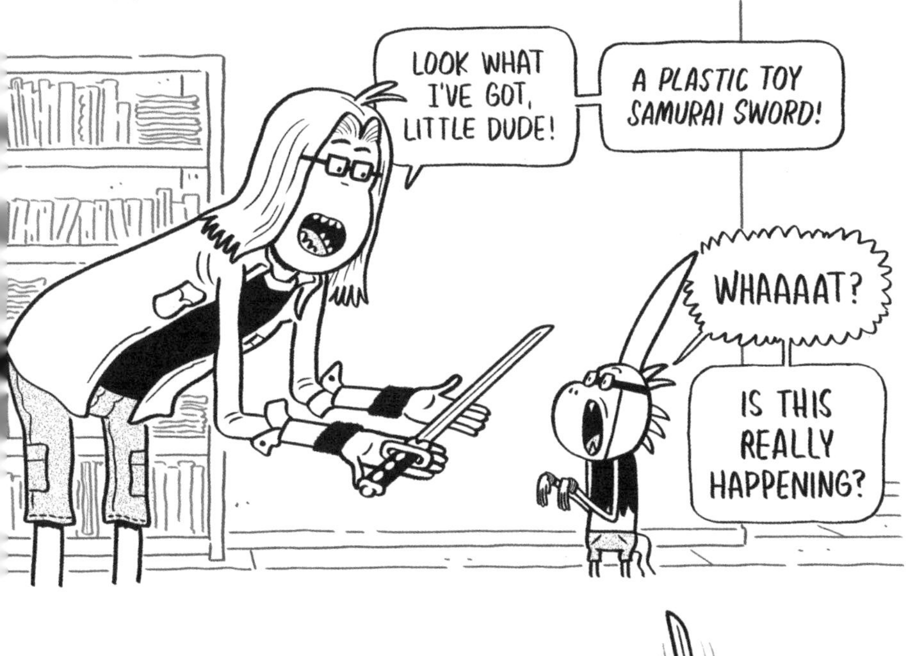
LOOK WHAT I'VE GOT, LITTLE DUDE!
A PLASTIC TOY SAMURAI SWORD!
WHAAAAT?
IS THIS REALLY HAPPENING?

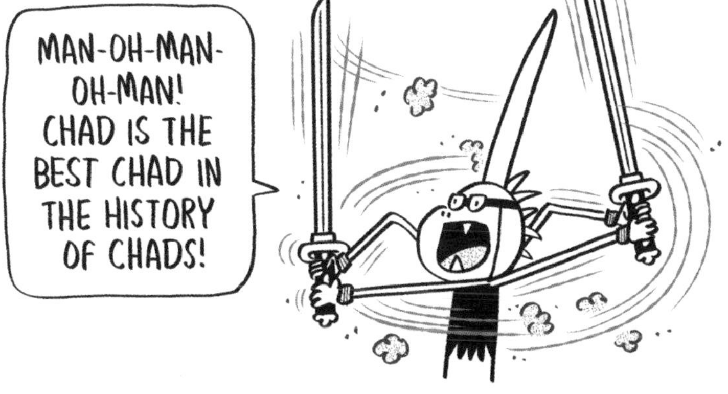
MAN-OH-MAN-OH-MAN! CHAD IS THE BEST CHAD IN THE HISTORY OF CHADS!

And Lizárdo's right — Chad IS the best Chad in the history of Chads. And I'm not just saying that because Chad lets me:

READ COMICS for breakfast,

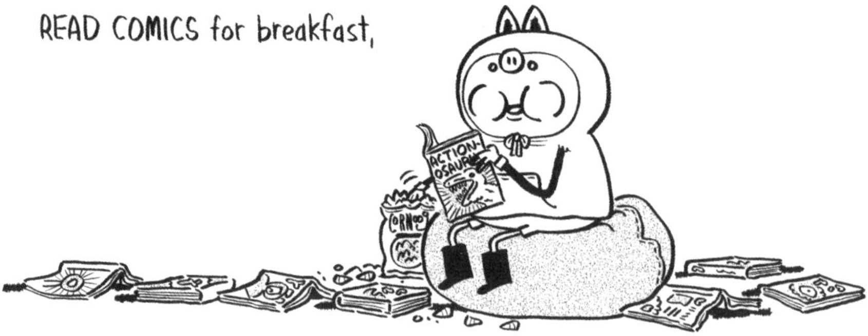
ACTION-

WATCH ANIME for lunch,

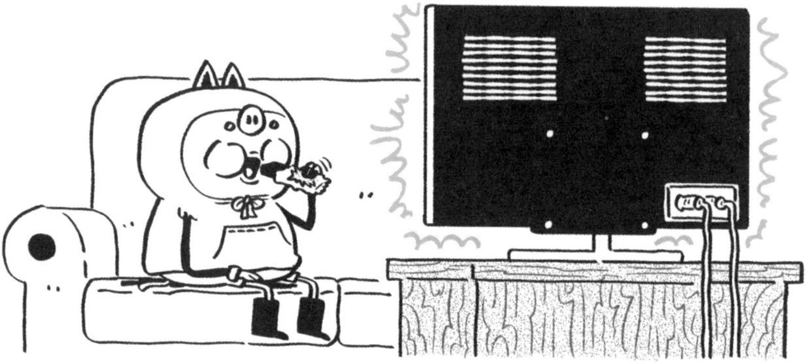

and EAT SUGAR-FROSTED SUGAR DONUTS for dinner.

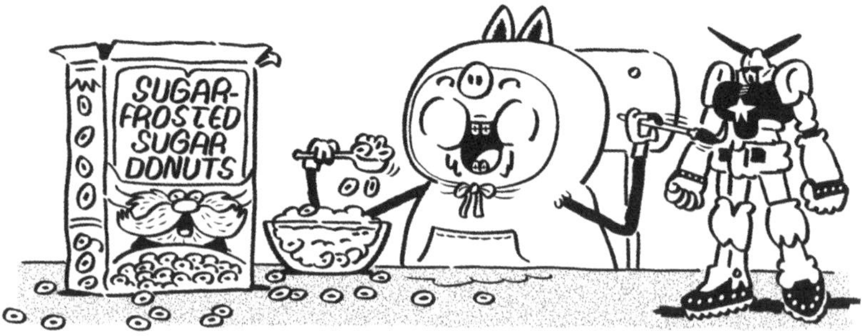
SUGAR-FROSTED SUGAR DONUTS

WHICH IS WHY, on my Human Type Person Rating System, I give Chad five out of five stars.

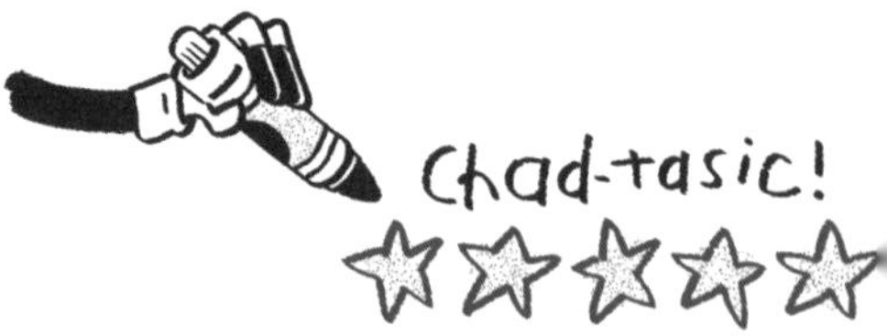
Chad-tasic!

Yes, our new freelance pet gig was INCREDIBLE. That is, until I found out there was ANOTHER pet living in Chad's apartment.

This I found out while reading Shark Detective #29. 'Cause right in the middle of a big Shark Detective battle scene, an ominous hamster — in an ominous hamster ball — rolled in — with an ominous warning:

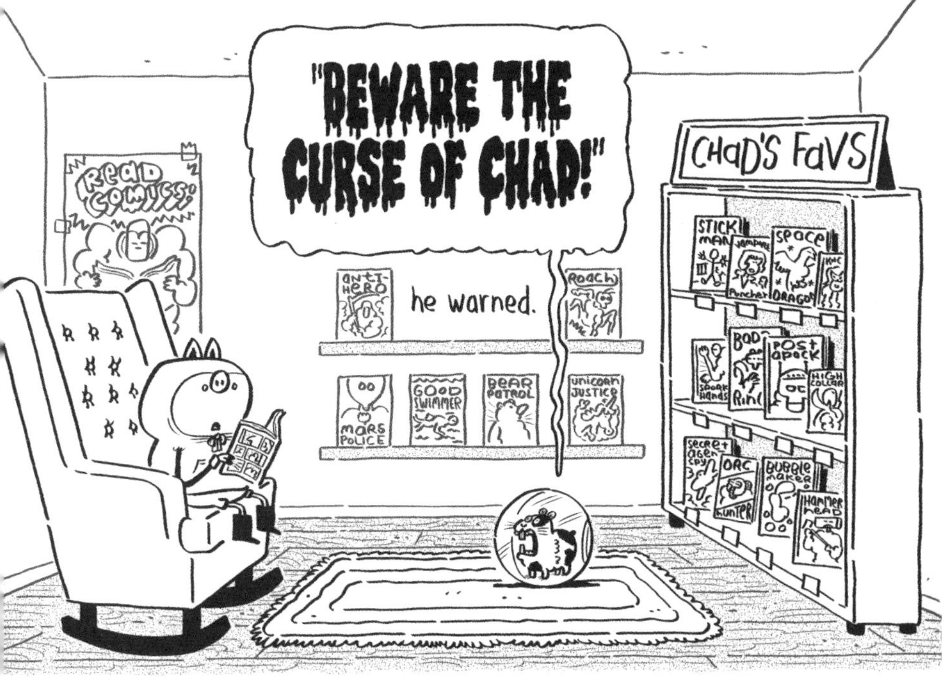
"BEWARE THE CURSE OF CHAD!"
he warned.
CHAD'S FAVS
ANTI-HERO
ROACH
MARS POLICE
GOOD SWIMMER
BEAR PATROL
UNICORN JUSTICE
STICK MAN
SPACE
POST APOCK
ORC HUNTER
BUBBLE MAKER
HAMMER HEAD

As far as ominous hamsters go, this one was extra ominous-y.

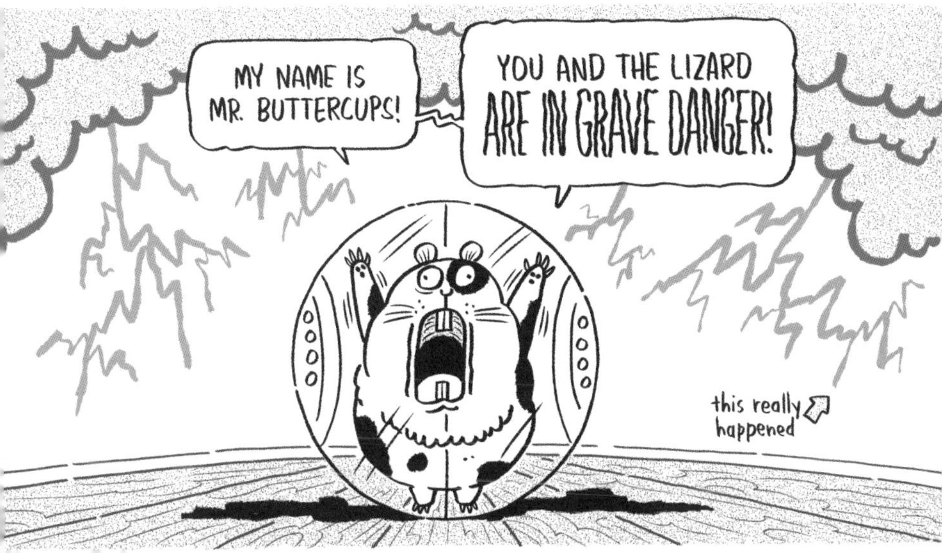
MY NAME IS MR. BUTTERCUPS!
YOU AND THE LIZARD ARE IN GRAVE DANGER!
this really happened

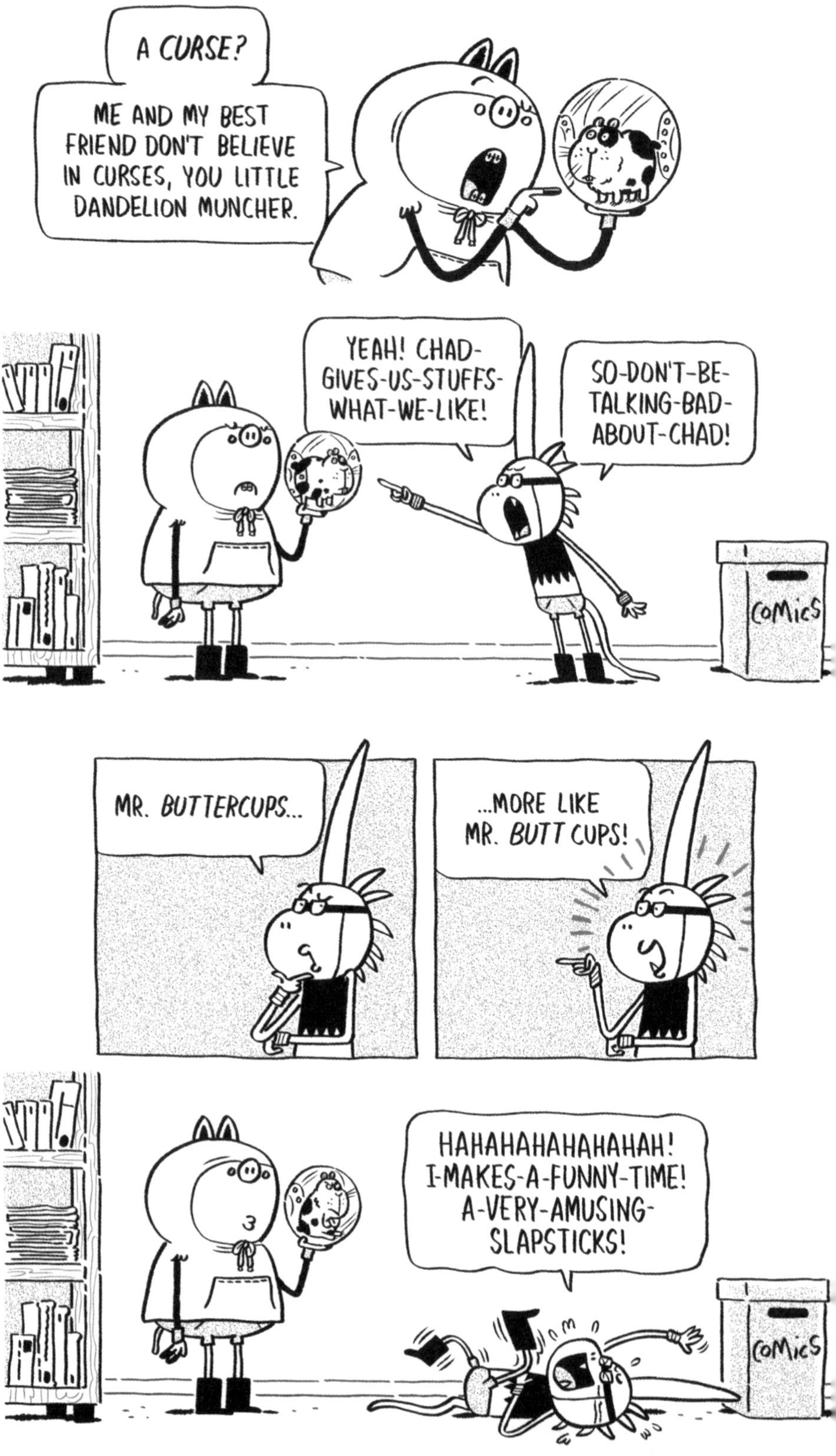
A CURSE?
ME AND MY BEST FRIEND DON'T BELIEVE IN CURSES, YOU LITTLE DANDELION MUNCHER.
YEAH! CHAD-GIVES-US-STUFFS-WHAT-WE-LIKE!
SO-DON'T-BE-TALKING-BAD-ABOUT-CHAD!
COMICS
MR. BUTTERCUPS...
...MORE LIKE MR. BUTT CUPS!
HAHAHAHAHAHAHAH! I-MAKES-A-FUNNY-TIME! A-VERY-AMUSING-SLAPSTICKS!
COMICS

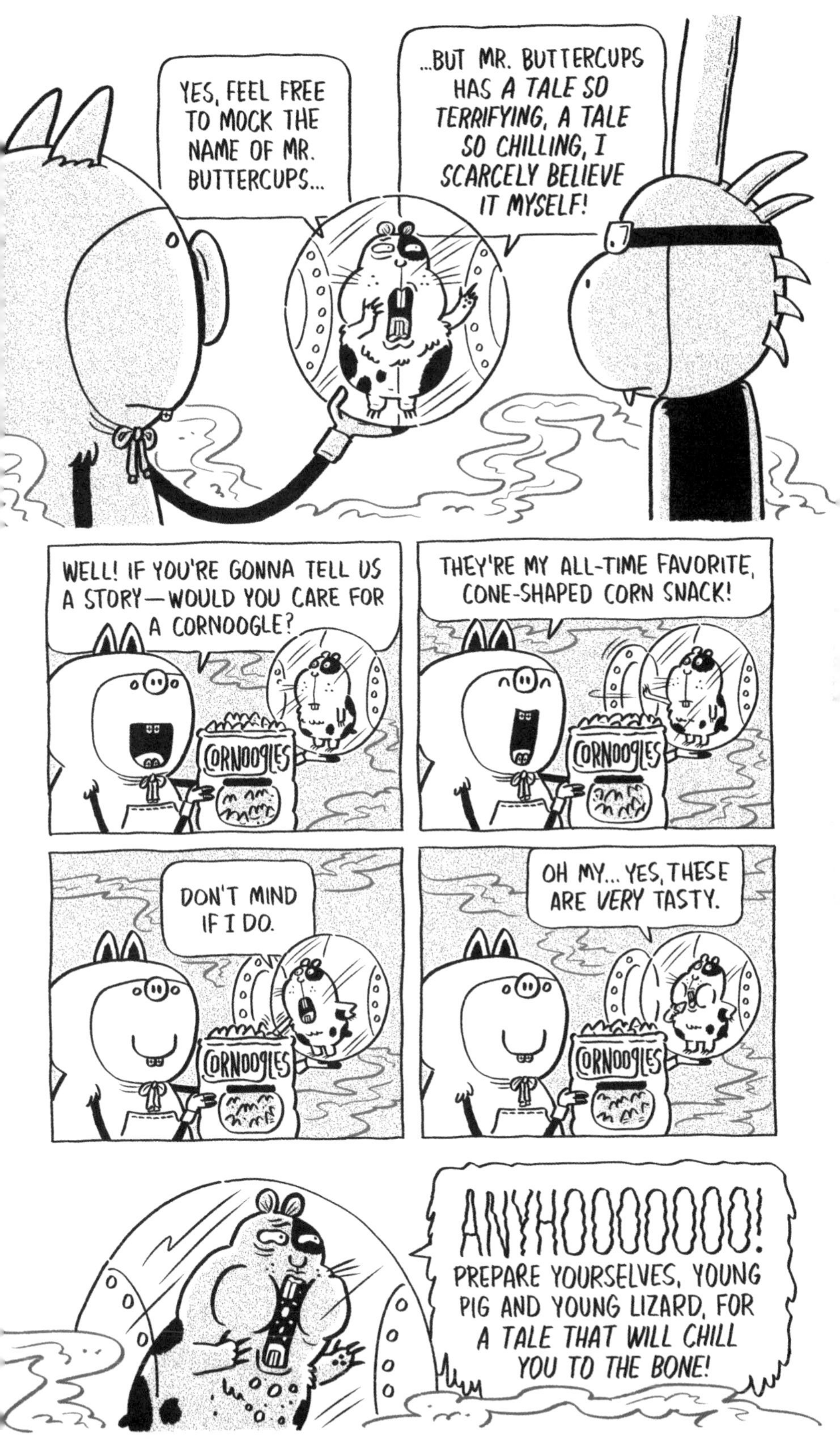
YES, FEEL FREE TO MOCK THE NAME OF MR. BUTTERCUPS...
...BUT MR. BUTTERCUPS HAS A TALE SO TERRIFYING, A TALE SO CHILLING, I SCARCELY BELIEVE IT MYSELF!
WELL! IF YOU'RE GONNA TELL US A STORY—WOULD YOU CARE FOR A CORNOOGLE?
CORNOOGLES
THEY'RE MY ALL-TIME FAVORITE, CONE-SHAPED CORN SNACK!
CORNOOGLES
DON'T MIND IF I DO.
CORNOOGLES
OH MY... YES, THESE ARE VERY TASTY.
CORNOOGLES
ANYHOOOOOOO!
PREPARE YOURSELVES, YOUNG PIG AND YOUNG LIZARD, FOR A TALE THAT WILL CHILL YOU TO THE BONE!

MR. BUTTERCUPS' BONE-CHILLING TALE

"Long, long ago—last month," said Mr. Buttercups, "I was a happy, carefree hamster. I came to Chad's apartment by way of PetJoy, America's #1 Pet Superstore. I remember how I used to frolic in my little hamster wheel. Oh, how I loved TO FROLIC! Couldn't get enough of THE FROLICKING!"

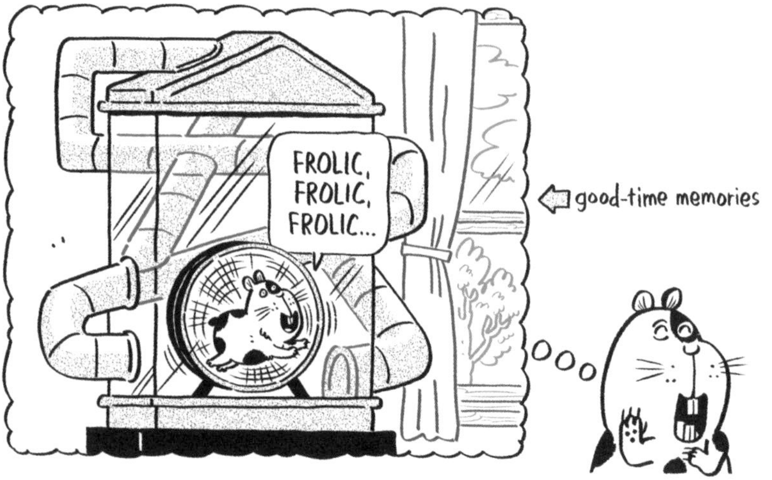
FROLIC, FROLIC, FROLIC...
good-time memories

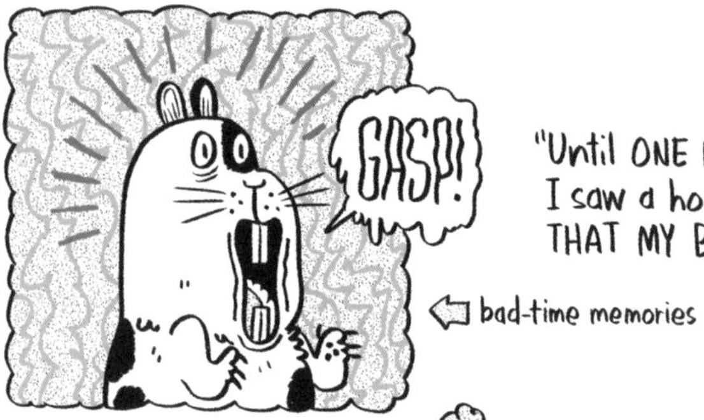
GASP!
bad-time memories

"Until ONE NIGHT when I saw a horror so horrific THAT MY BLOOD RAN COLD!"

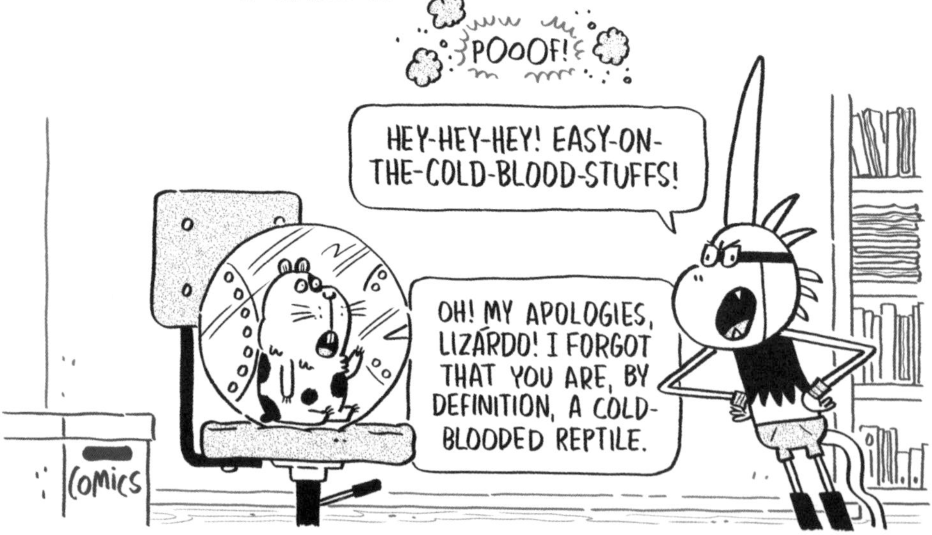
POOOF!
HEY-HEY-HEY! EASY-ON-THE-COLD-BLOOD-STUFFS!
OH! MY APOLOGIES, LIZARDO! I FORGOT THAT YOU ARE, BY DEFINITION, A COLD-BLOODED REPTILE.
COMICS

"Anyhoo— it was a night of a full moon," continued Mr. Buttercups. "Which I was gazing at from the comfort of my little hamster wheel. SUDDENLY, when I glanced over my shoulder, I saw Chad transform from a comics-reading, anime-watching, model-building nerd into...

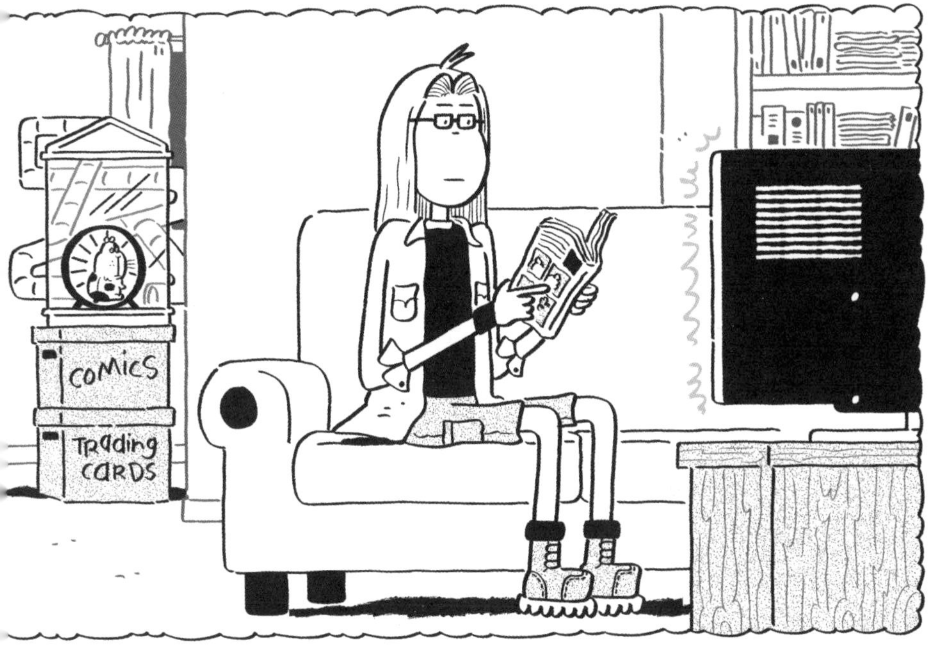
COMICS
TRADING CARDS

A WERE-CHAD!!!"

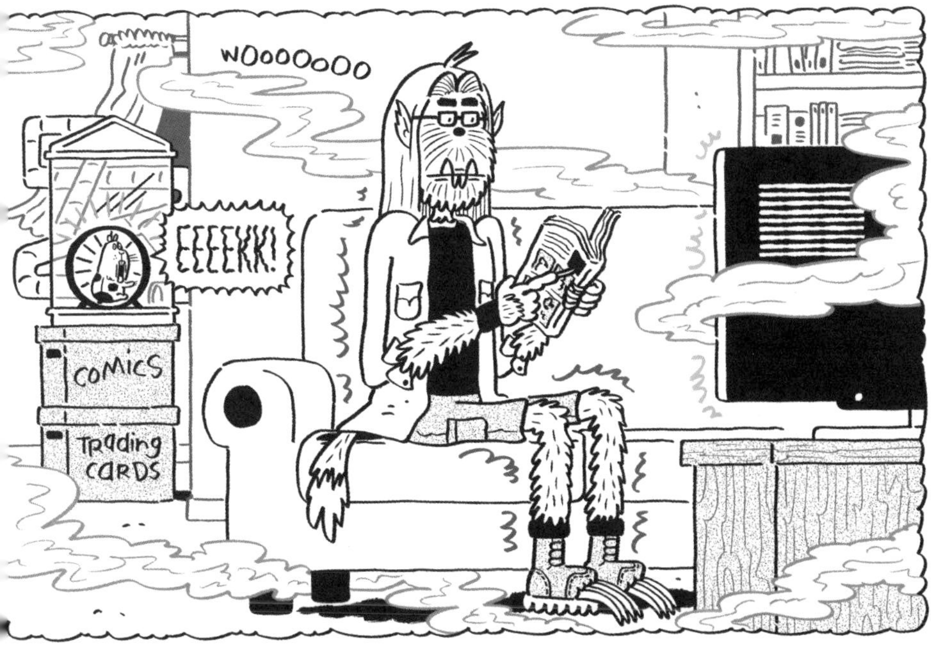
WOOOOOOO
EEEEKK!
COMICS
TRADING CARDS

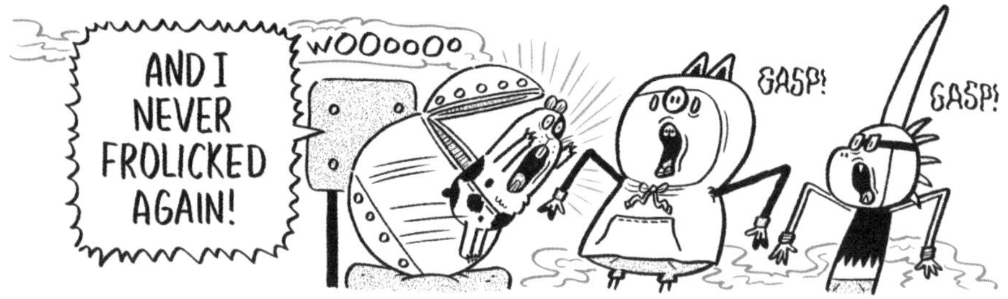
AND I NEVER FROLICKED AGAIN!
WOOOOOO
GASP!
GASP!

"But you're probably wondering about the Science," said Mr. Buttercups. "So lemme explain. You see, Chad was born the 7th Chad of a 7th Chad. Which means that when Chad sees the light of a full moon, an Ancient Family Curse causes him to transform into a half-wolf, half-Chad monster!"

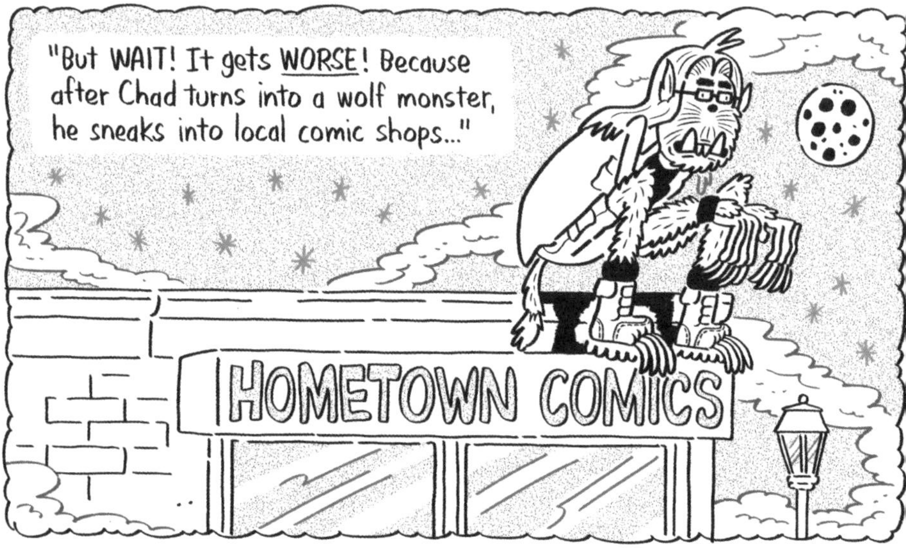
"But WAIT! It gets WORSE! Because after Chad turns into a wolf monster, he sneaks into local comic shops..."
HOMETOWN COMICS

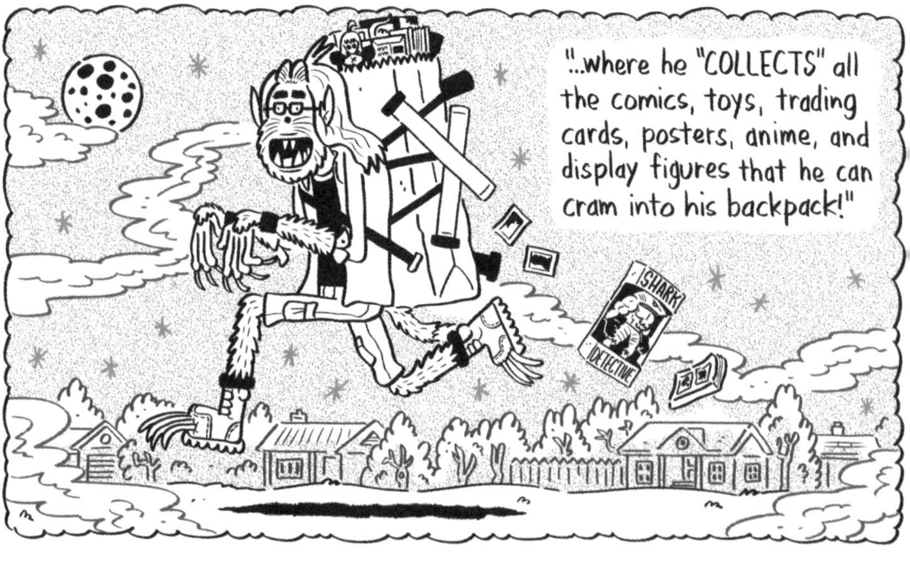
"...where he "COLLECTS" all the comics, toys, trading cards, posters, anime, and display figures that he can cram into his backpack!"
SHARK
DETECTIVE

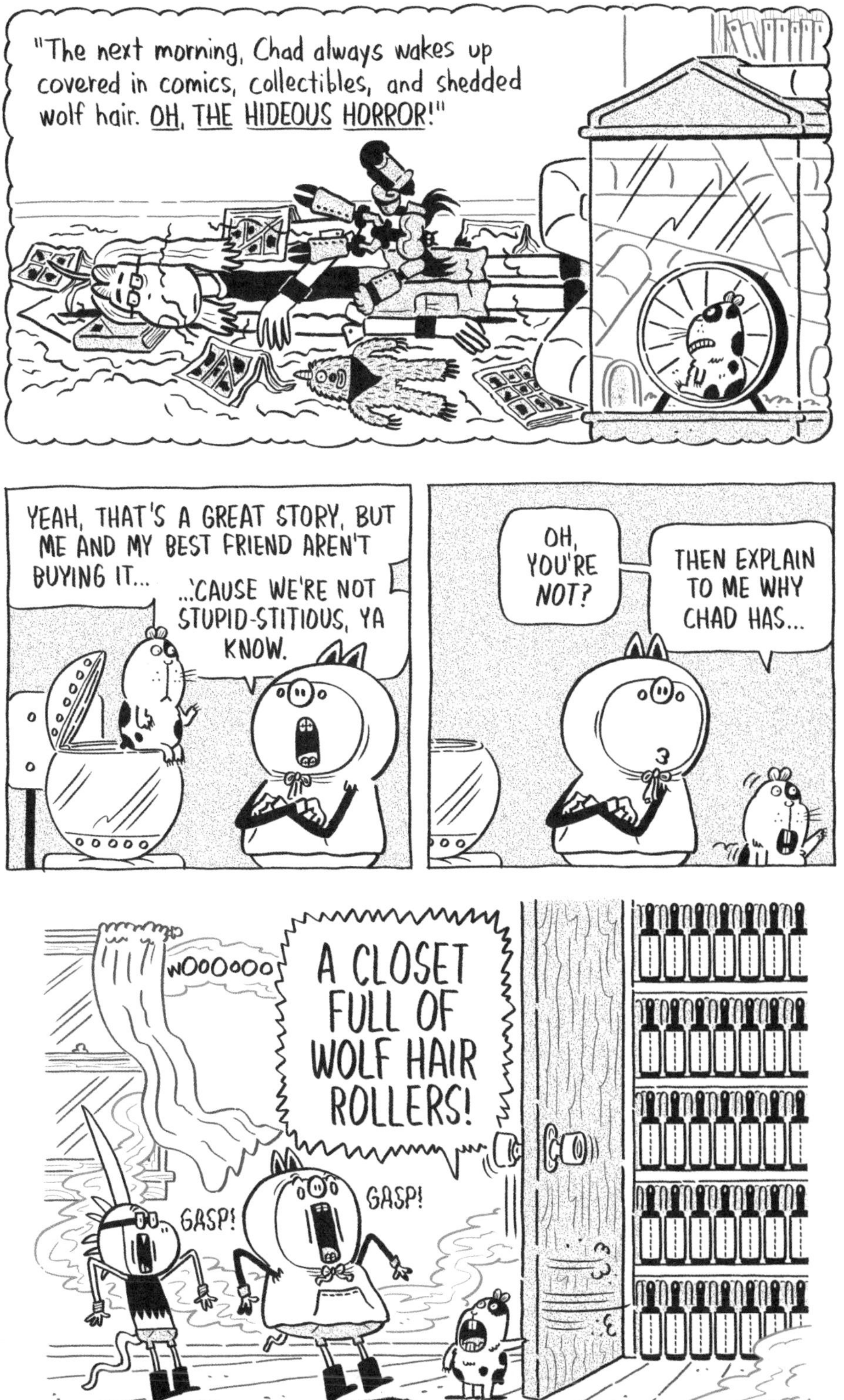
"The next morning, Chad always wakes up covered in comics, collectibles, and shedded wolf hair. OH, THE HIDEOUS HORROR!"
YEAH, THAT'S A GREAT STORY, BUT ME AND MY BEST FRIEND AREN'T BUYING IT...
...'CAUSE WE'RE NOT STUPID-STITIOUS, YA KNOW.
OH, YOU'RE NOT?
THEN EXPLAIN TO ME WHY CHAD HAS...
WOOOOOO
A CLOSET FULL OF WOLF HAIR ROLLERS!
GASP!
GASP!

I won't lie. Mr. Buttercups' story was really freaking me out. Comic-collecting werewolves? The 7th Chad of a 7th Chad? These are not super happy thoughts. And ALSO — why did Mr. Buttercups have to tell us all this JUST AS a creepy moon was rising over the horizon?

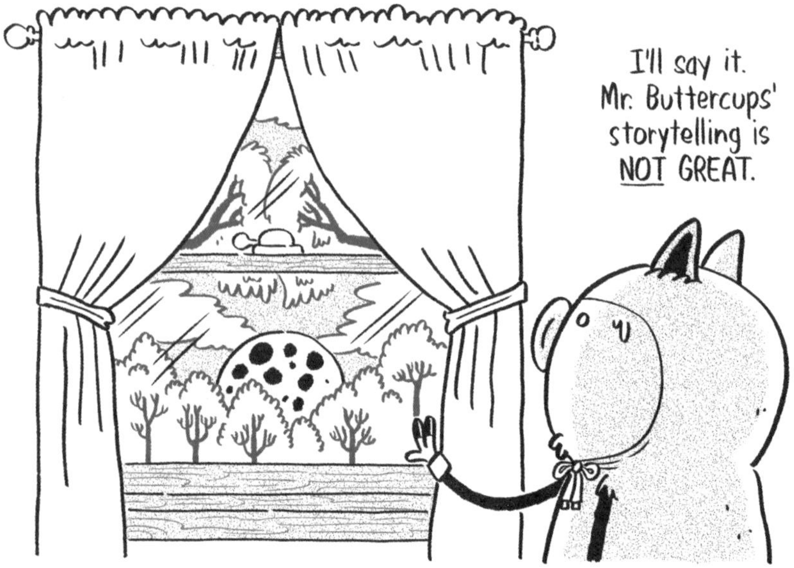
I'll say it.
Mr. Buttercups' storytelling is NOT GREAT.

"Oh. I forgot to mention," mentioned Mr. Buttercups. "CRAZY thing happened to me. You see, right after Chad turned into that wolf thingy, Were-Chad thought I was a hot dog and bit me on the bottom bits. Well, long story short, the moon instantly transformed me into...

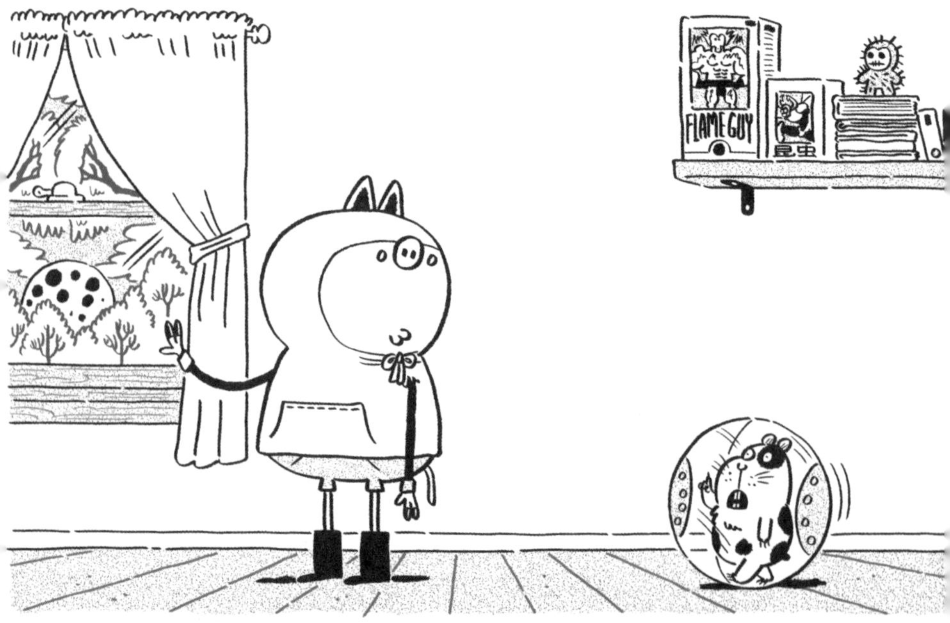
FLAMEGUY

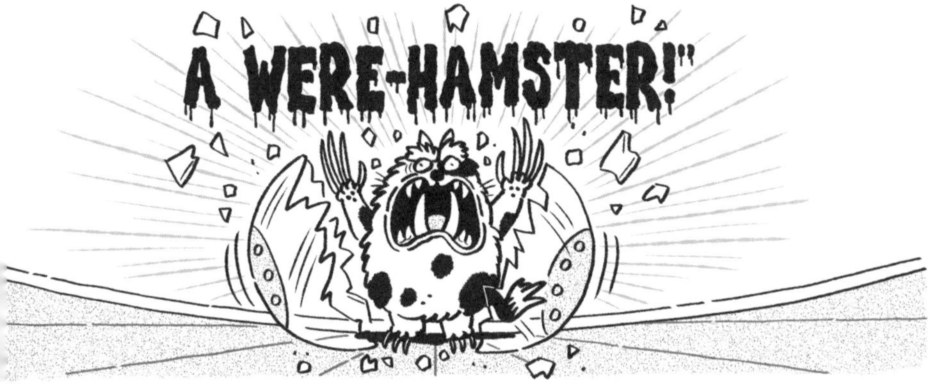
A WERE-HAMSTER!"

And before you could say HOT DOG GONE WRONG, I was in a life-or-death struggle with a vicious, bloodthirsty rodent.

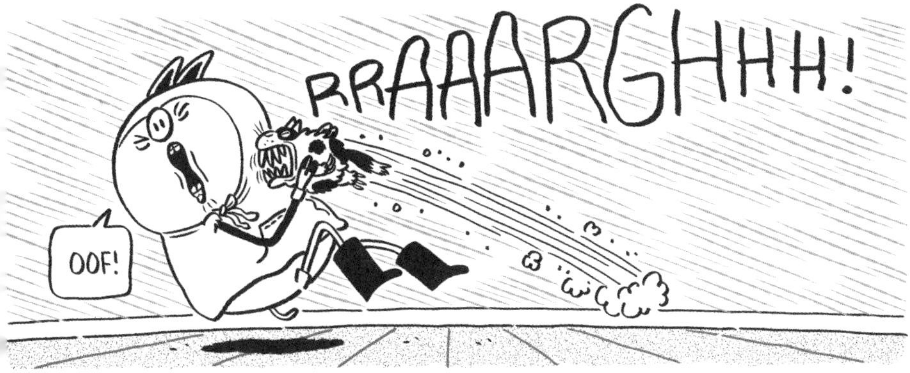
RRAAARGHHH!
OOF!

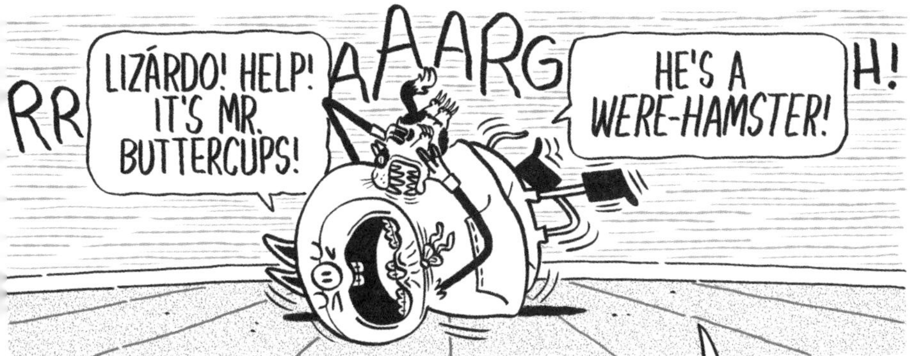
RRAAARGH!
LIZÁRDO! HELP! IT'S MR. BUTTERCUPS!
HE'S A WERE-HAMSTER!

I yelled for Lizárdo, but he couldn't hear me 'cause he was wearing headphones and practicing his ULTIMATE SAMURAI BATTLE MOVES.

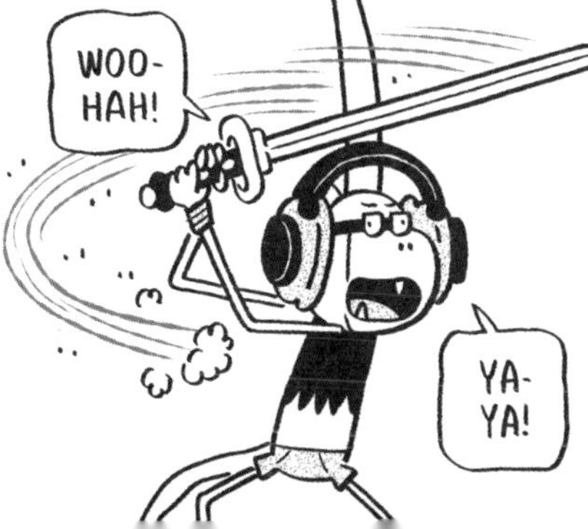
WOO-HAH!
YA-YA!

The next thing I remembered was waking up on a fresh pile of comic books. Could I be? Was I a? And why couldn't I? Finish a sentence?

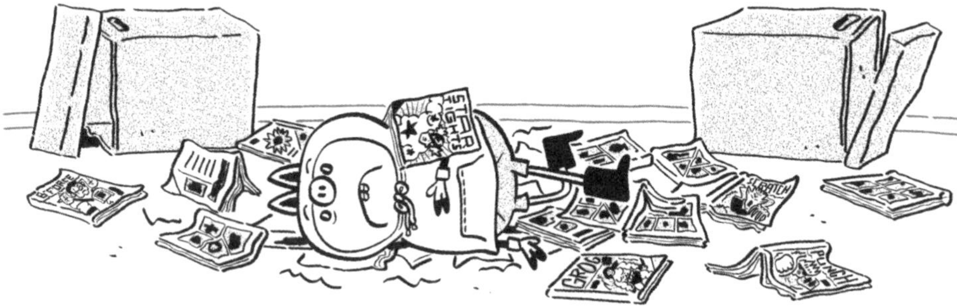

When I looked in the bathroom mirror, I saw a horror so horrible, a horror so hideous THAT MY BLOOD RAN COLD.*

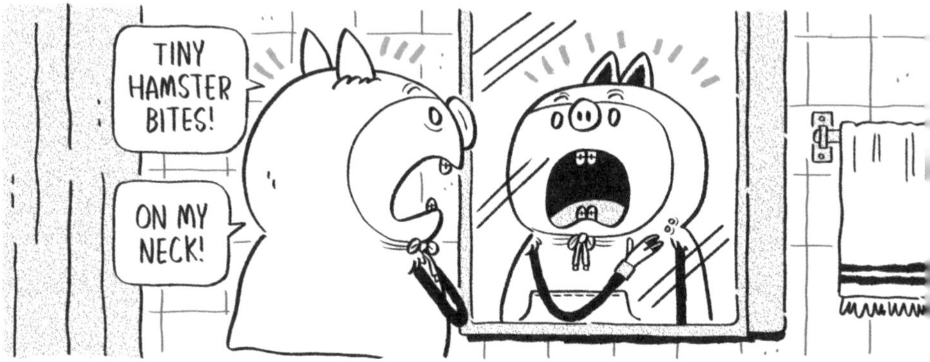
TINY HAMSTER BITES!
ON MY NECK!

Yep. The true fact of the matter was that:

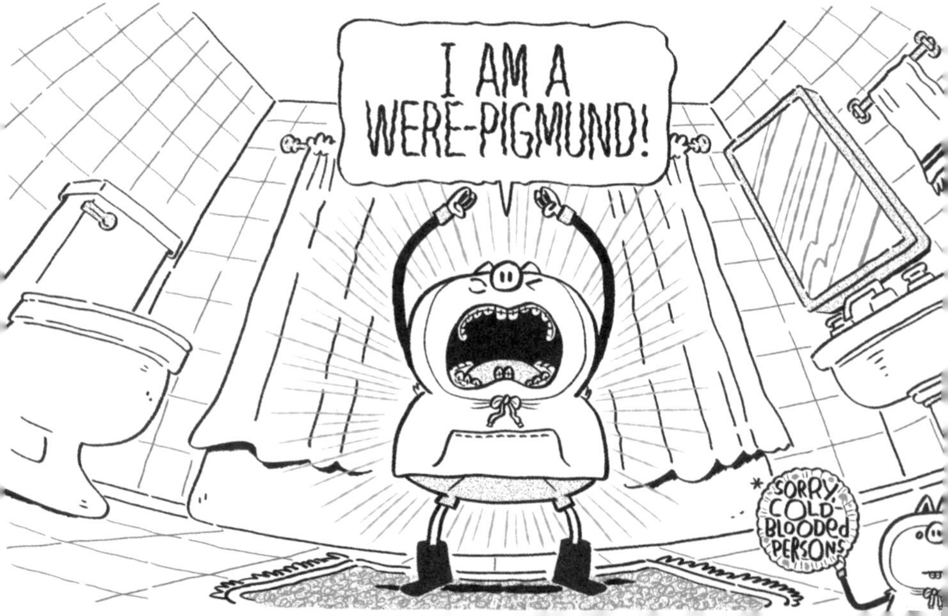
I AM A WERE-PIGMUND!
* SORRY, COLD-BLOODED PERSONS.

CURSE OF THE WERE-PIG

I won't lie. Knowing that on the next full moon, you're going to turn into a hideous wolf monster really CHANGES you. I was no longer the happy, carefree pig I used to be. All I ever do anymore is:

sit in a DARK ROOM,

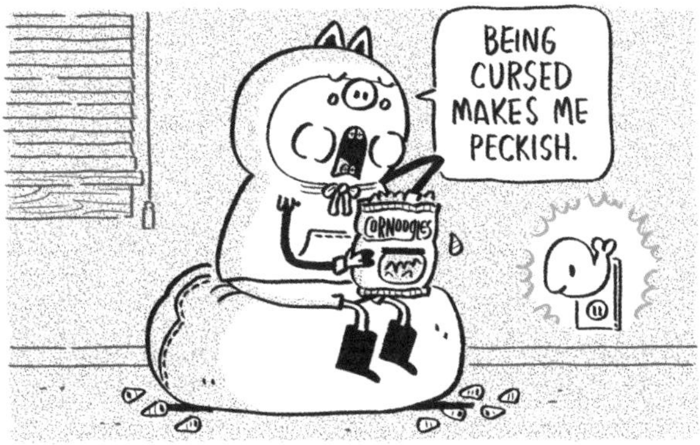
BEING CURSED MAKES ME PECKISH.
CORNOODLES

write DARK POETRY,

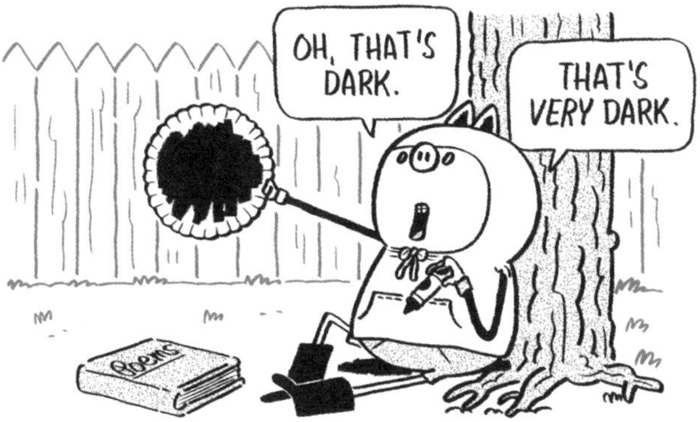
OH, THAT'S DARK.
THAT'S VERY DARK.
Poems

and get DARK TATTOOS. (Like this dark tattoo I drew in washable magic markers while sitting in front of a mirror, which is why LONE WOLF looks like ƎNO⅃ ꟻ⅃OW.)

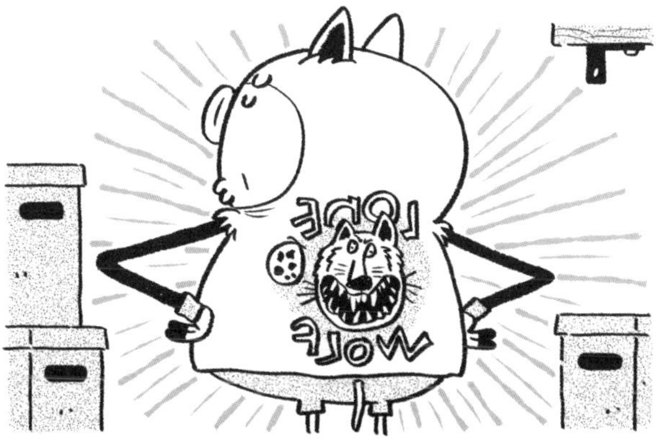

When the big day of the next full moon arrived, I knew what I had to do. I had to SAVE my best friend Lizárdo.

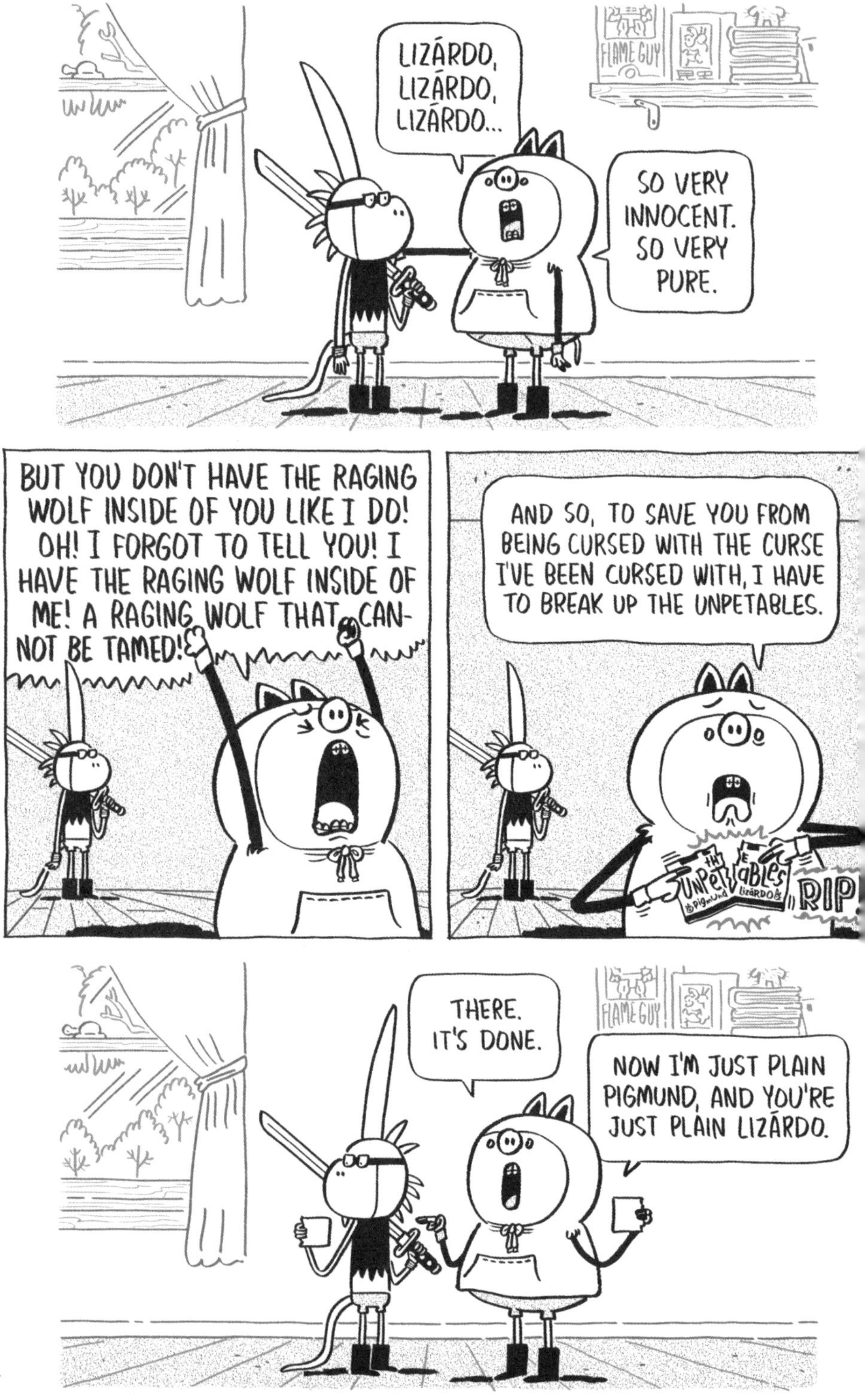
FLAME GUY
LIZÁRDO, LIZÁRDO, LIZÁRDO...
SO VERY INNOCENT. SO VERY PURE.
BUT YOU DON'T HAVE THE RAGING WOLF INSIDE OF YOU LIKE I DO! OH! I FORGOT TO TELL YOU! I HAVE THE RAGING WOLF INSIDE OF ME! A RAGING WOLF THAT CAN-NOT BE TAMED!
AND SO, TO SAVE YOU FROM BEING CURSED WITH THE CURSE I'VE BEEN CURSED WITH, I HAVE TO BREAK UP THE UNPETABLES.
RIP
FLAME GUY
THERE. IT'S DONE.
NOW I'M JUST PLAIN PIGMUND, AND YOU'RE JUST PLAIN LIZÁRDO.

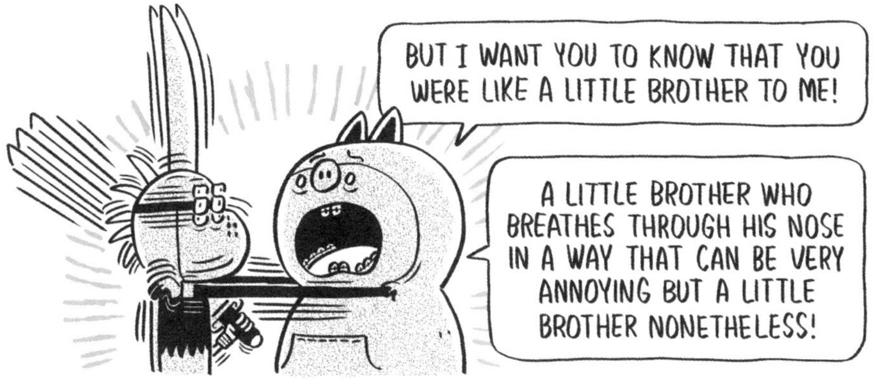
BUT I WANT YOU TO KNOW THAT YOU WERE LIKE A LITTLE BROTHER TO ME!
A LITTLE BROTHER WHO BREATHES THROUGH HIS NOSE IN A WAY THAT CAN BE VERY ANNOYING BUT A LITTLE BROTHER NONETHELESS!

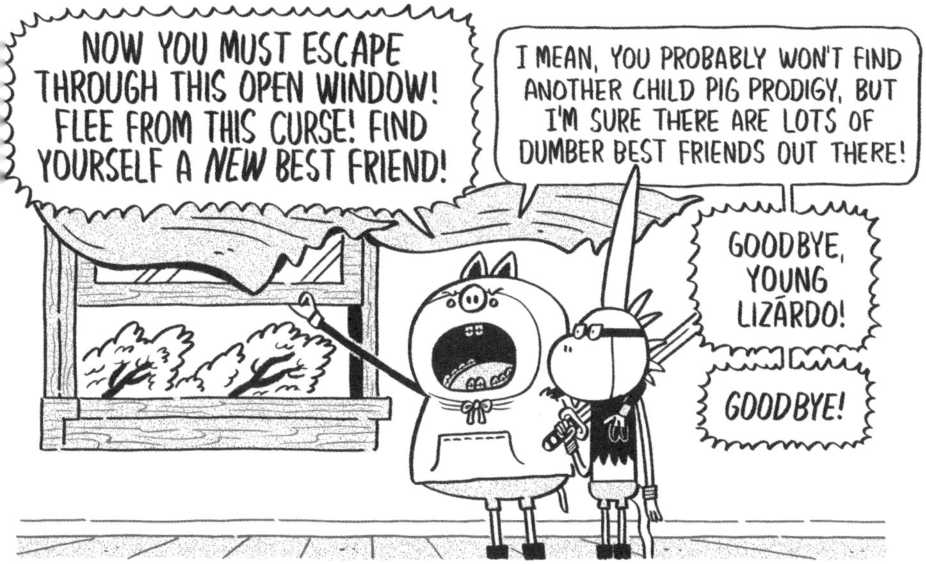
NOW YOU MUST ESCAPE THROUGH THIS OPEN WINDOW! FLEE FROM THIS CURSE! FIND YOURSELF A *NEW* BEST FRIEND!
I MEAN, YOU PROBABLY WON'T FIND ANOTHER CHILD PIG PRODIGY, BUT I'M SURE THERE ARE LOTS OF DUMBER BEST FRIENDS OUT THERE!
GOODBYE, YOUNG LIZÁRDO!
GOODBYE!

And with that, I walked out of Lizárdo's life FOREVER. Oh. I forgot to mention. As I walked out of Lizárdo's life forever, I turned and LOOKED BACK. Lizárdo was obviously in DEEP, DEEP PAIN.

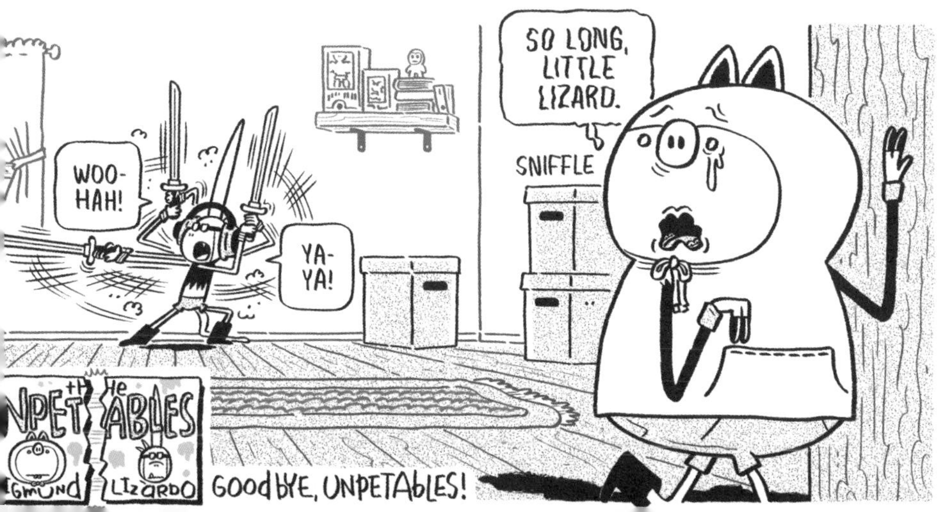
WOO-HAH!
YA-YA!
SO LONG, LITTLE LIZARD.
SNIFFLE
GOODBYE, UNPETABLES!

The Unpetables were broken up, and in a few hours, I would turn into a hideous wolf. In other words, I was having a REALLY bad day. And so, while I waited to turn into a monster, I curled up on the couch and watched season 6 of Zombie Smoosher Z — which is REALLY good, by the way.

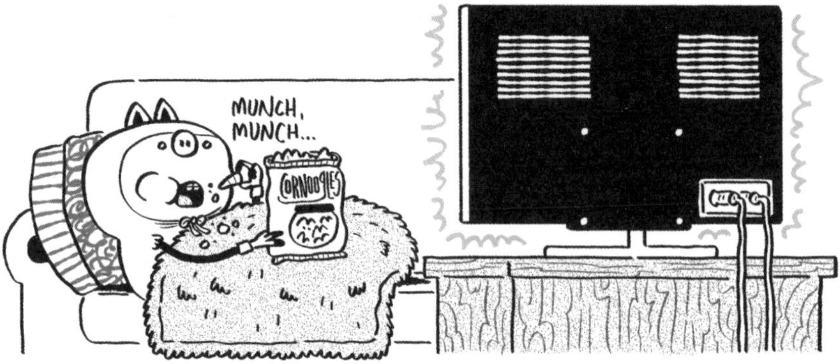
MUNCH,
MUNCH...
CORNOOGLES

Then, as multiple zombies were being smooshed, I choked on a Cornoogle.

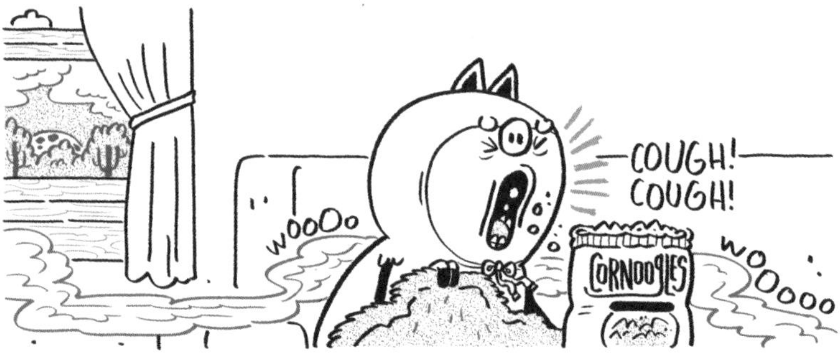
wOOOo
COUGH!
COUGH!
CORNOOGLES
WOOoooo

Is this the part? Where I turn? Into a Were-Pigmund?

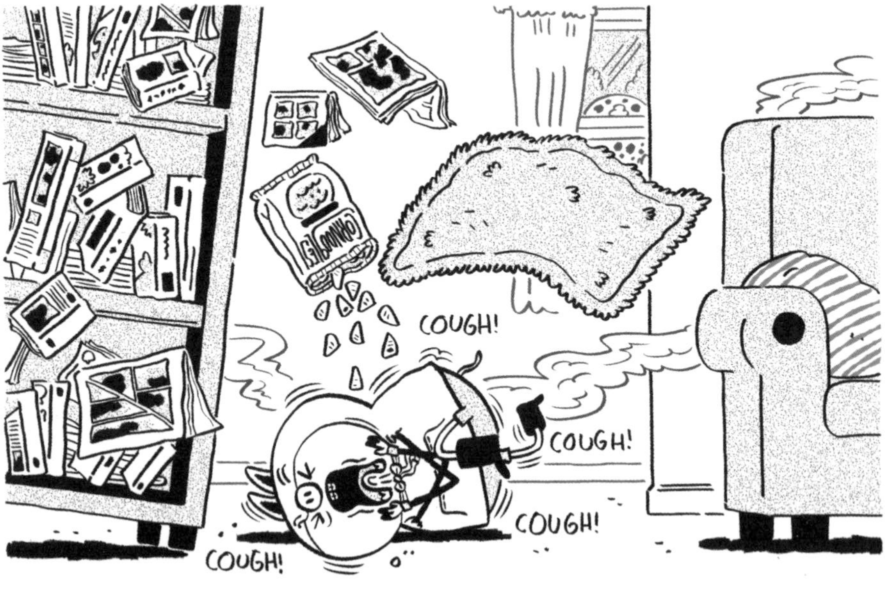
COUGH!
COUGH!
COUGH!
COUGH!

Why, yes.

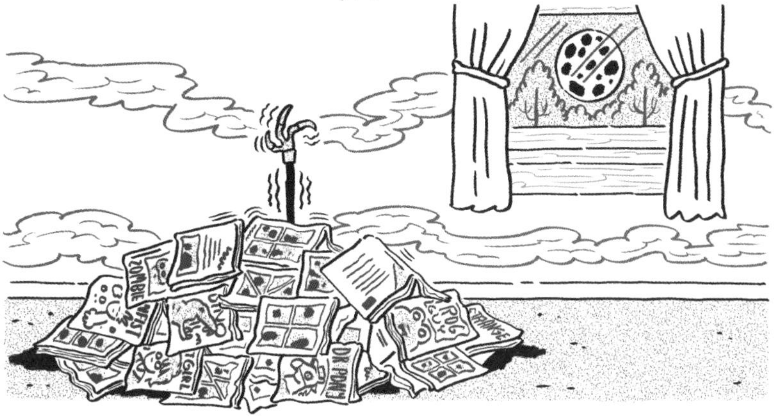

Yes, it is.

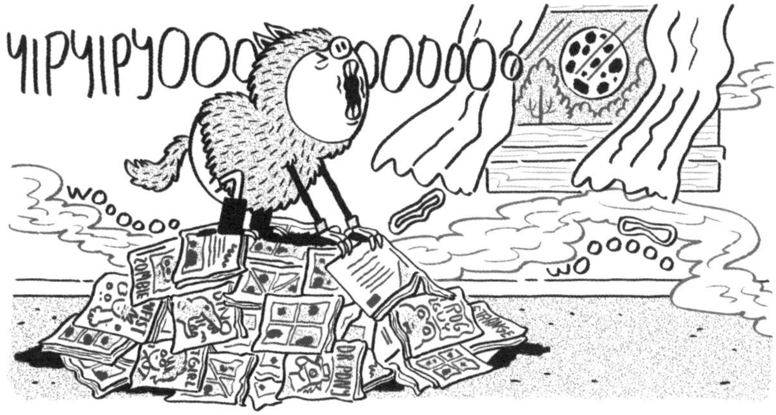
YIPYIPYOOOOOOOOOO
WOoooooo
WOoooooo

AND SO —
this is me being cursed by
the Curse of the Were-pig—

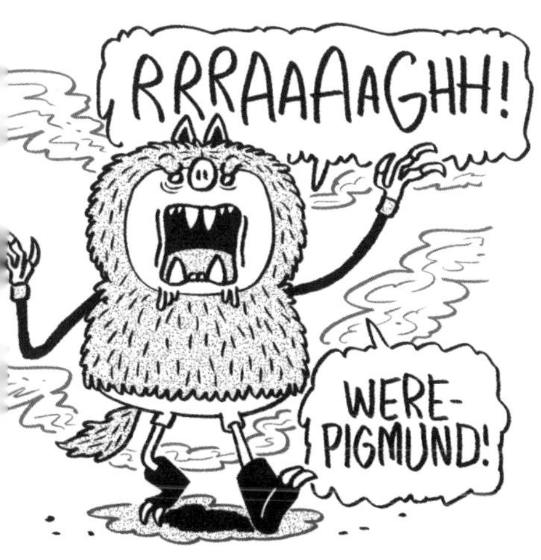
RRRAAAAGHH!
WERE-PIGMUND!

and also, a pretty
bad case of fleas.

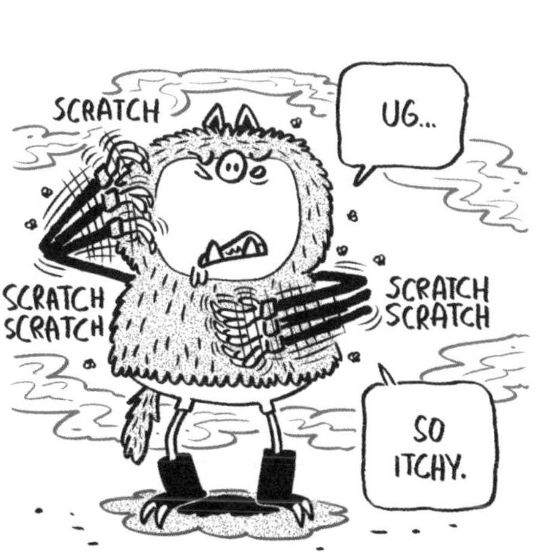
SCRATCH
UG...
SCRATCH SCRATCH
SCRATCH SCRATCH
SO ITCHY.

But I was not alone in my horrible hideousness.
I had two horrible, hideous roommates.

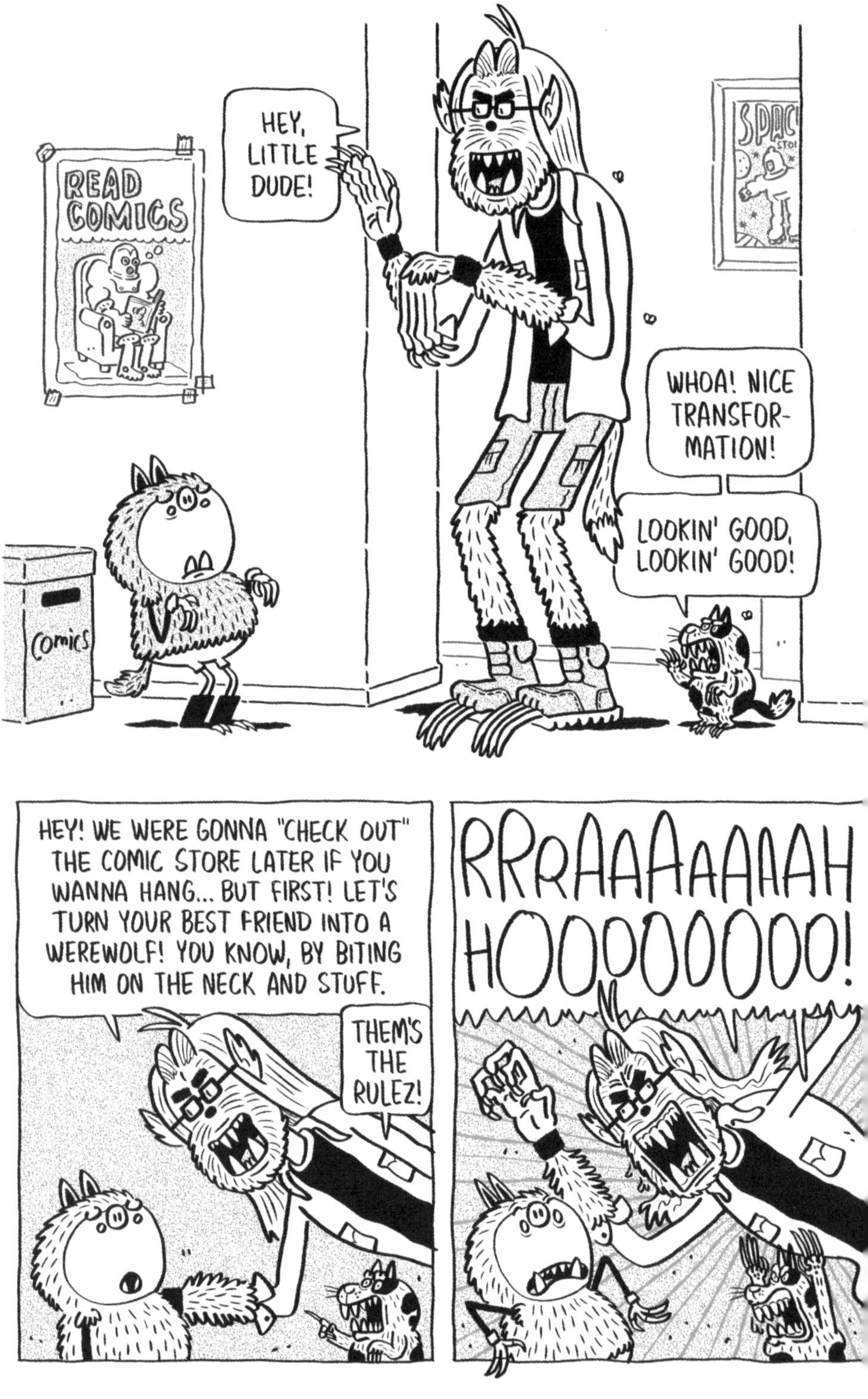

READ COMICS
HEY, LITTLE DUDE!
WHOA! NICE TRANSFOR-MATION!
LOOKIN' GOOD, LOOKIN' GOOD!
Comics
HEY! WE WERE GONNA "CHECK OUT" THE COMIC STORE LATER IF YOU WANNA HANG... BUT FIRST! LET'S TURN YOUR BEST FRIEND INTO A WEREWOLF! YOU KNOW, BY BITING HIM ON THE NECK AND STUFF.
THEM'S THE RULEZ!
RRRAAAAAAAAH HOOOOOOOO!

LITTLE DID I KNOW that Lizárdo didn't escape like I told him to. Instead, he was waiting with WEREWOLF REPELLENT that he made by pouring garlic, vinegar, rotten eggs, and stinky cheese into a Super Soaker Water Blaster.

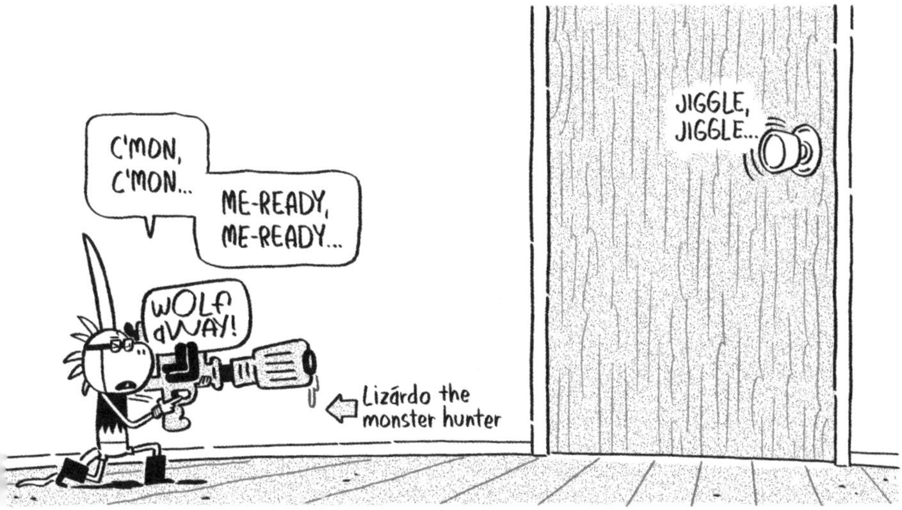
C'MON,
C'MON...
ME-READY,
ME-READY...
WOLF AWAY!
Lizárdo the monster hunter
JIGGLE,
JIGGLE...

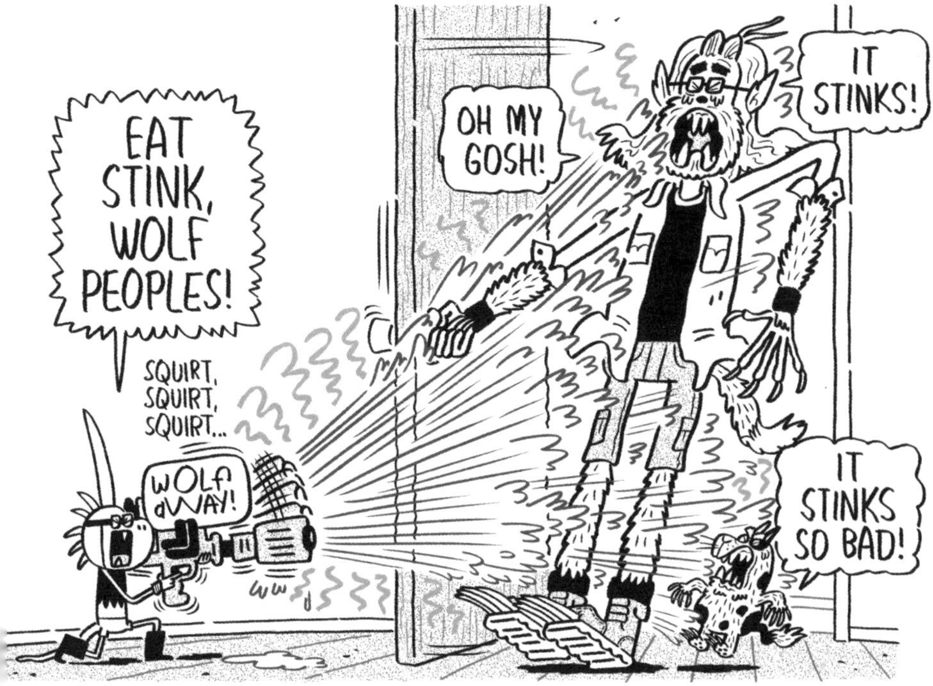
EAT STINK, WOLF PEOPLES!
SQUIRT, SQUIRT, SQUIRT...
WOLF AWAY!
OH MY GOSH!
IT STINKS!
IT STINKS SO BAD!

SCIENCE FACT: The stink receptors in a wolf's nose are 10,000 times more ensitive than the stink receptors in a human's. AND SO, to the average were-olf, Lizárdo's repellent would STINK with a STINK of UNBEARABLE STINKINESS.

WHICH IS WHY my were-roommates RAN LIKE CRAZY to escape Lizárdo's stink-tacular stink-fest.

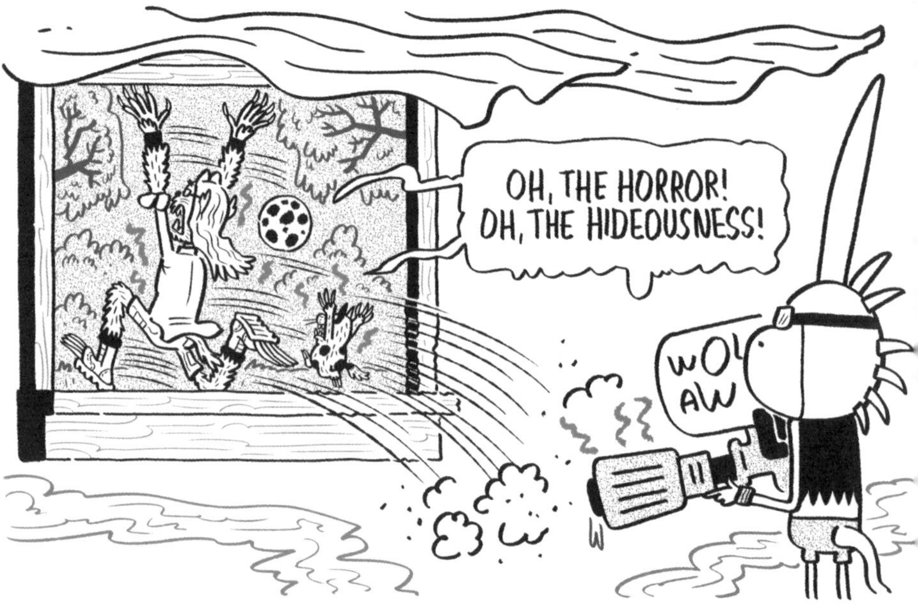

OH, THE HORROR! OH, THE HIDEOUSNESS!

WHERE WAS I, you ask? Well, if you must know, I was in the were-bathroom. (What? You don't think that hideous wolf monsters gotta go, too?) ANYHOW, by the time I washed my hands and combed my hair, Lizárdo was ALL OUT of werewolf repellent.

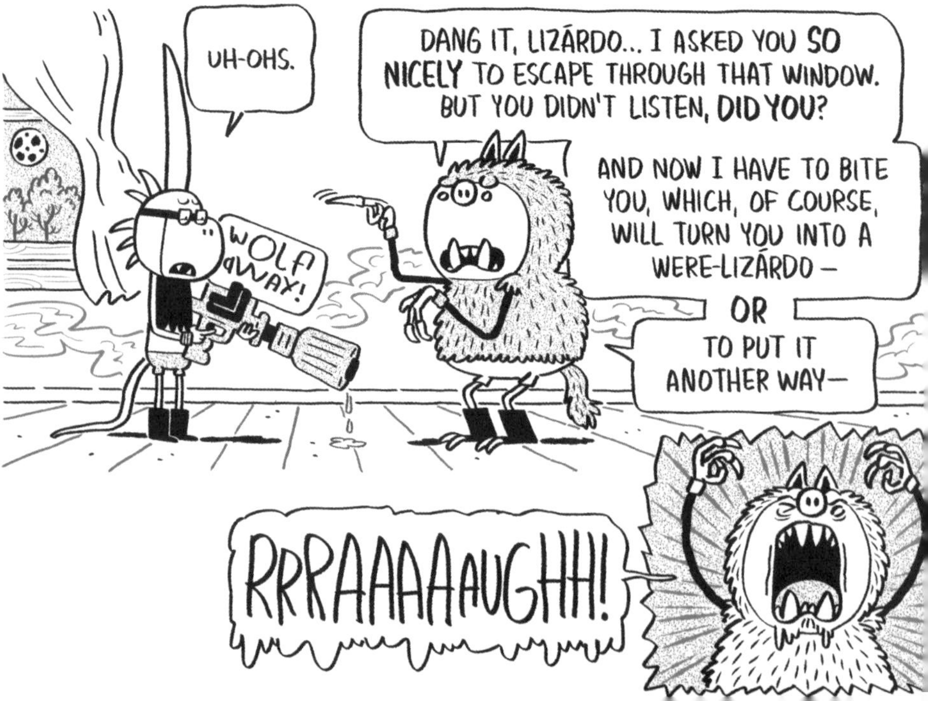

UH-OHS.
DANG IT, LIZÁRDO... I ASKED YOU SO NICELY TO ESCAPE THROUGH THAT WINDOW. BUT YOU DIDN'T LISTEN, DID YOU?
AND NOW I HAVE TO BITE YOU, WHICH, OF COURSE, WILL TURN YOU INTO A WERE-LIZÁRDO —
OR
TO PUT IT ANOTHER WAY—
WOLF AWAY!
RRRAAAAAUGHH!

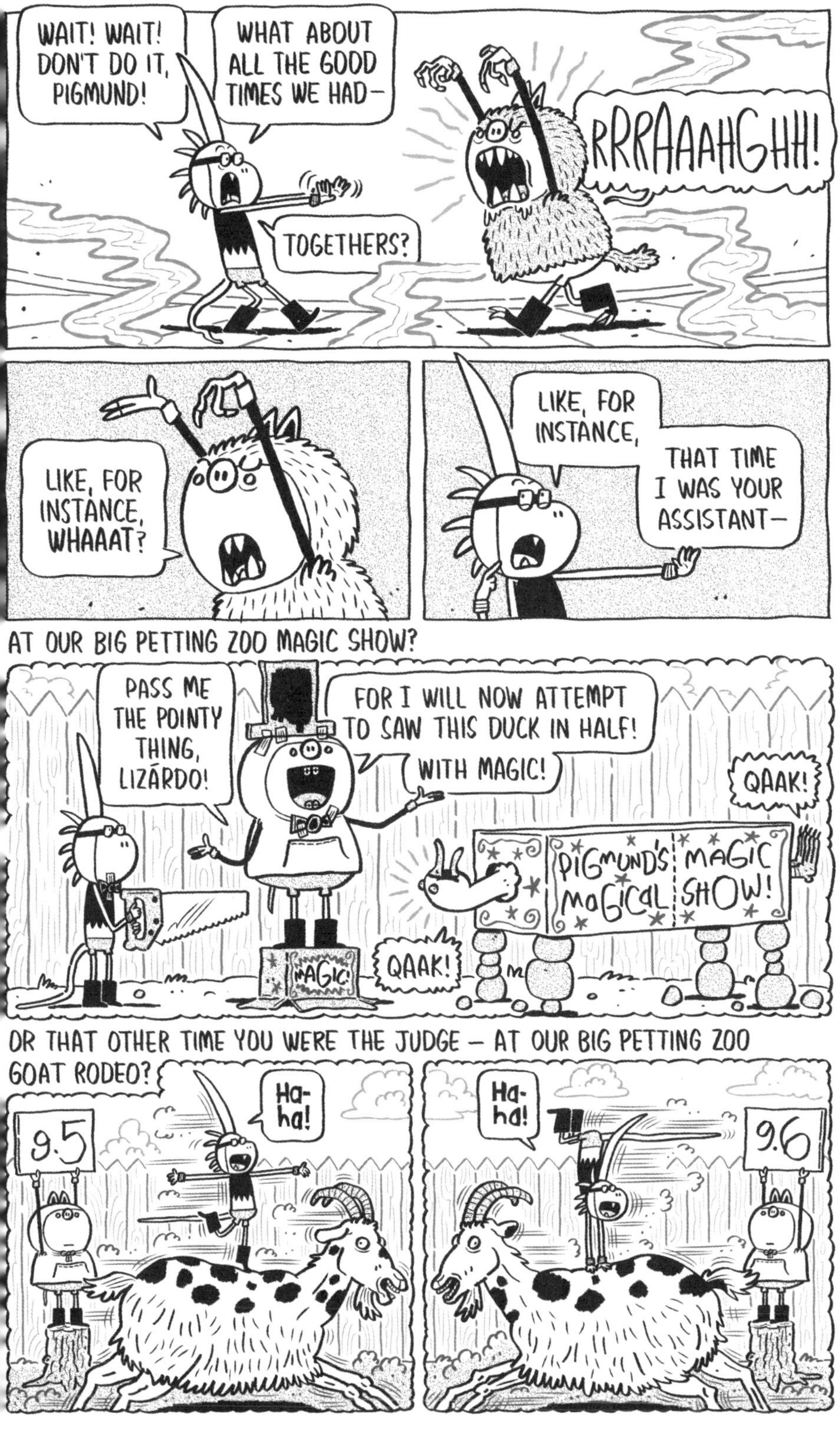
WAIT! WAIT! DON'T DO IT, PIGMUND!
WHAT ABOUT ALL THE GOOD TIMES WE HAD—
TOGETHERS?
RRRAAAHGHH!
LIKE, FOR INSTANCE, WHAAAT?
LIKE, FOR INSTANCE,
THAT TIME I WAS YOUR ASSISTANT—
AT OUR BIG PETTING ZOO MAGIC SHOW?
PASS ME THE POINTY THING, LIZÁRDO!
FOR I WILL NOW ATTEMPT TO SAW THIS DUCK IN HALF!
WITH MAGIC!
QAAK!
PIGMUND'S MAGICAL MAGIC SHOW!
MAGIC
QAAK!
OR THAT OTHER TIME YOU WERE THE JUDGE — AT OUR BIG PETTING ZOO GOAT RODEO?
9.5
Ha-ha!
Ha-ha!
9.6

I won't lie. Lizárdo's good-time memories were CHANGING me. I guess that underneath all my horrible hideousness, my sensitive pig heart was pumping out THE WARM FUZZIES.

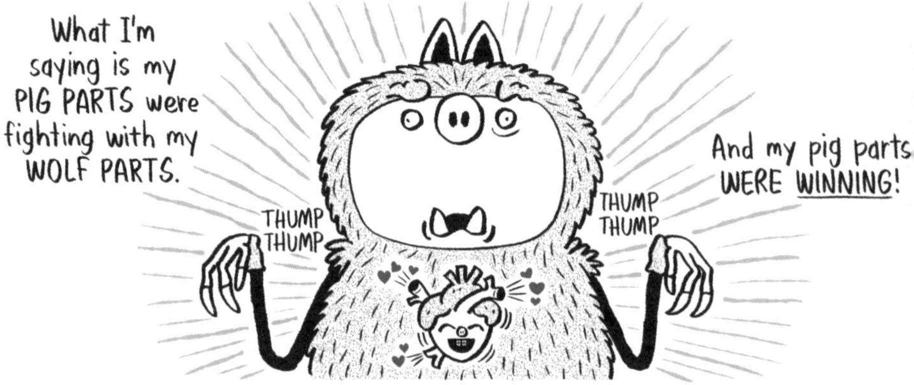
What I'm saying is my PIG PARTS were fighting with my WOLF PARTS.
THUMP THUMP
THUMP THUMP
And my pig parts WERE WINNING!

That is, until a Princess Mobile Suit action figure fell on my head.

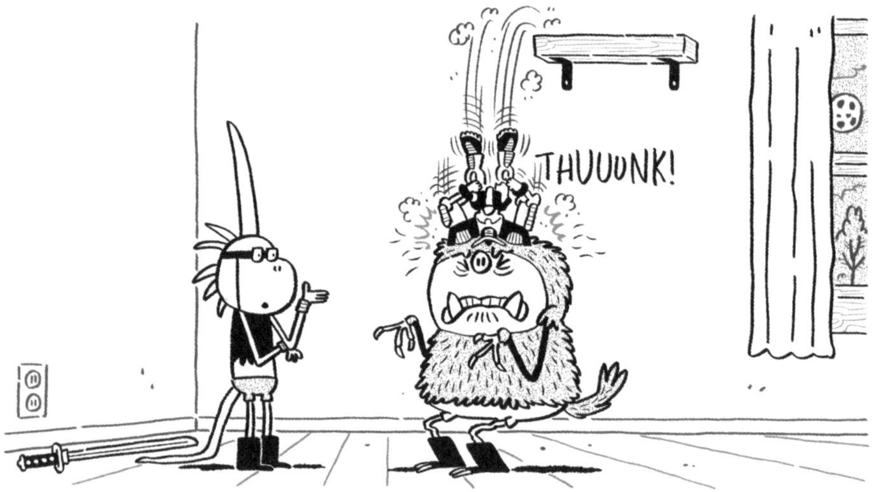
THUUUNK!

Which just made my wolf parts REALLY MAD.

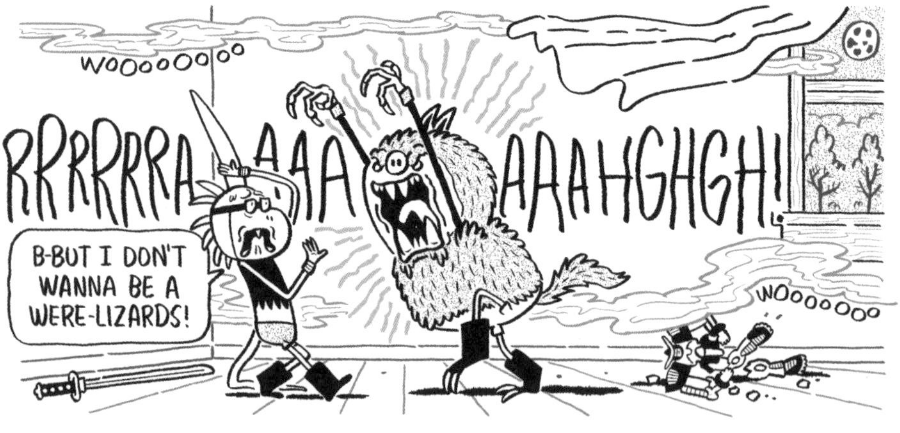
WOOOOOOOO
RRRRRRAAAAAAAHGHGH!
B-BUT I DON'T WANNA BE A WERE-LIZARDS!
WOOOOOOO

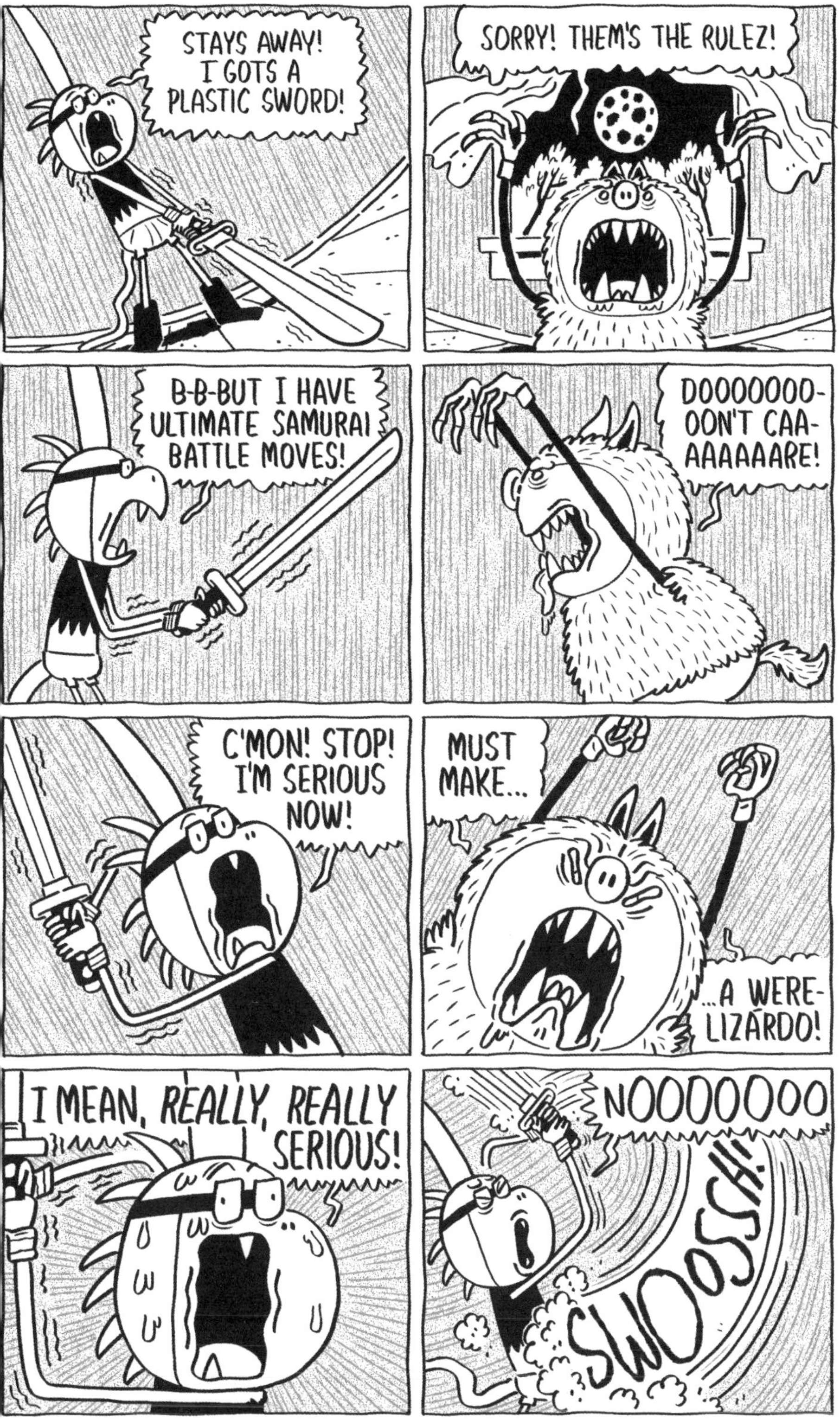
STAYS AWAY! I GOTS A PLASTIC SWORD!
SORRY! THEM'S THE RULEZ!
B-B-BUT I HAVE ULTIMATE SAMURAI BATTLE MOVES!
DOOOOOOO-OON'T CAA-AAAAAARE!
C'MON! STOP! I'M SERIOUS NOW!
MUST MAKE...
...A WERE-LIZARDO!
I MEAN, *REALLY, REALLY* SERIOUS!
NOOOOOOO
SWOOSCH!!

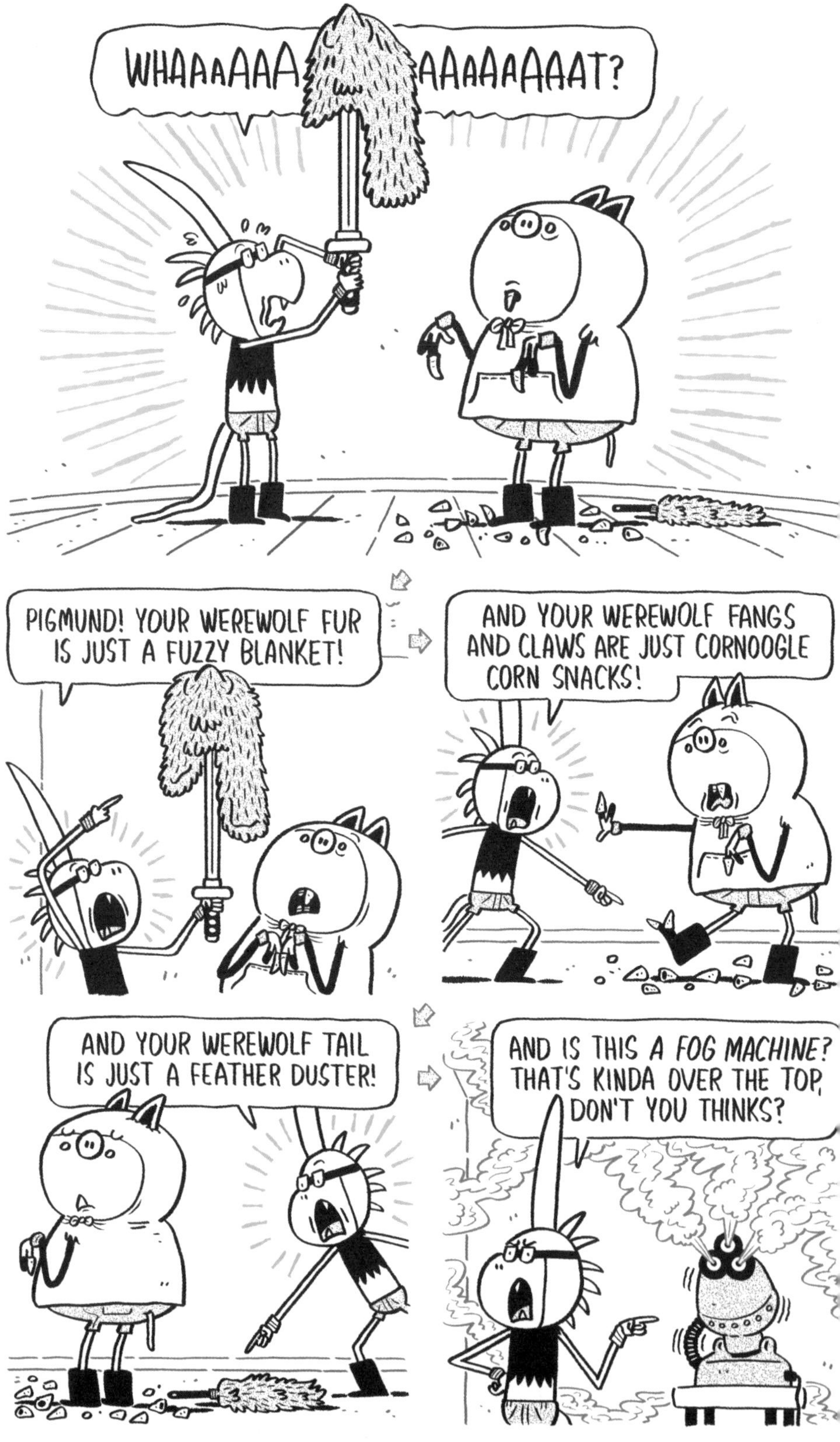
WHAAAAAA AAAAAAAAT?
PIGMUND! YOUR WEREWOLF FUR IS JUST A FUZZY BLANKET!
AND YOUR WEREWOLF FANGS AND CLAWS ARE JUST CORNOOGLE CORN SNACKS!
AND YOUR WEREWOLF TAIL IS JUST A FEATHER DUSTER!
AND IS THIS A *FOG MACHINE?* THAT'S KINDA OVER THE TOP, DON'T YOU THINKS?

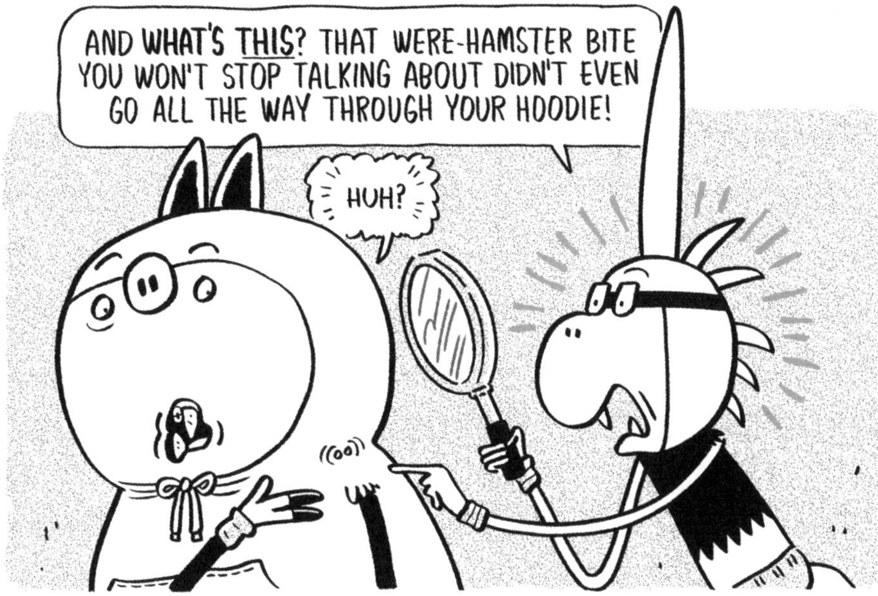
AND WHAT'S THIS? THAT WERE-HAMSTER BITE YOU WON'T STOP TALKING ABOUT DIDN'T EVEN GO ALL THE WAY THROUGH YOUR HOODIE!
HUH?

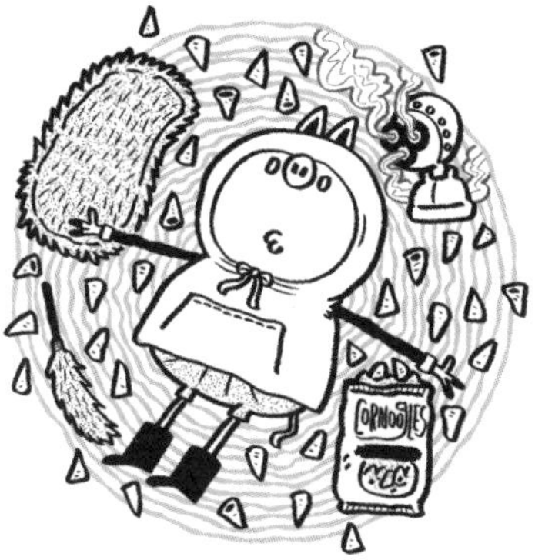
CORNOODLES

I won't lie.
THIS STORY
STOPPED MAKING
SENSE ABOUT
TWO PAGES AGO.
If I wasn't a?
Then how did I?
And what about the?

It was all so upsetting that I just —

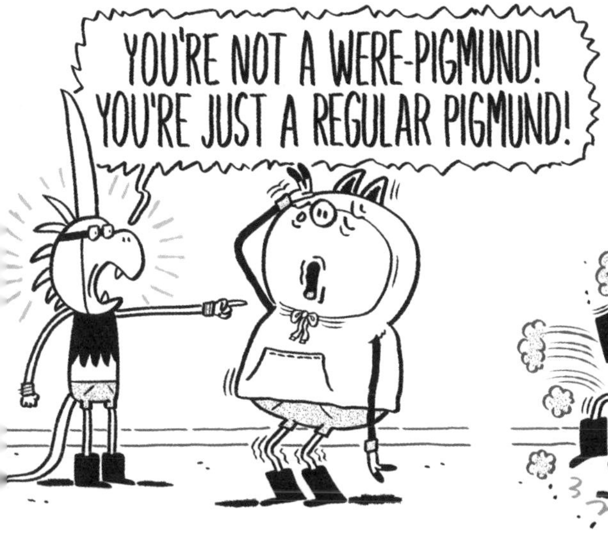
YOU'RE NOT A WERE-PIGMUND!
YOU'RE JUST A REGULAR PIGMUND!

FAINTED.

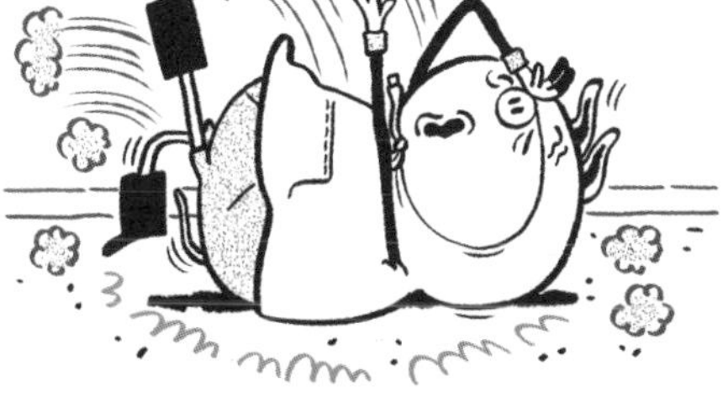
THUUNK!

A NEW DAY
The next morning, I woke up at the Hometown Animal Hospital For Animals.

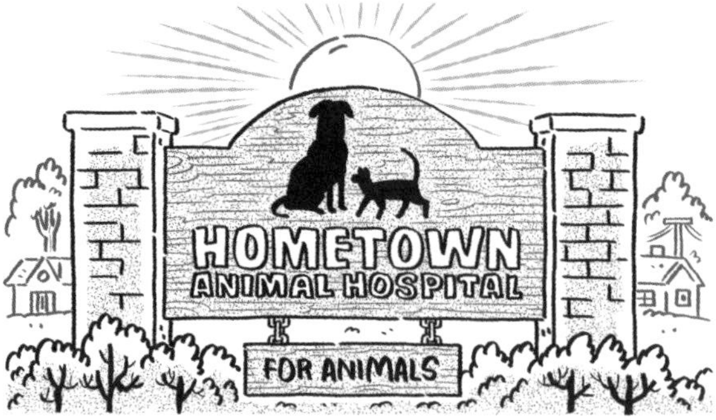
HOMETOWN
ANIMAL HOSPITAL
FOR ANIMALS

"You took a pretty nasty fall last night," said a veterinarian with a very important looking clipboard.

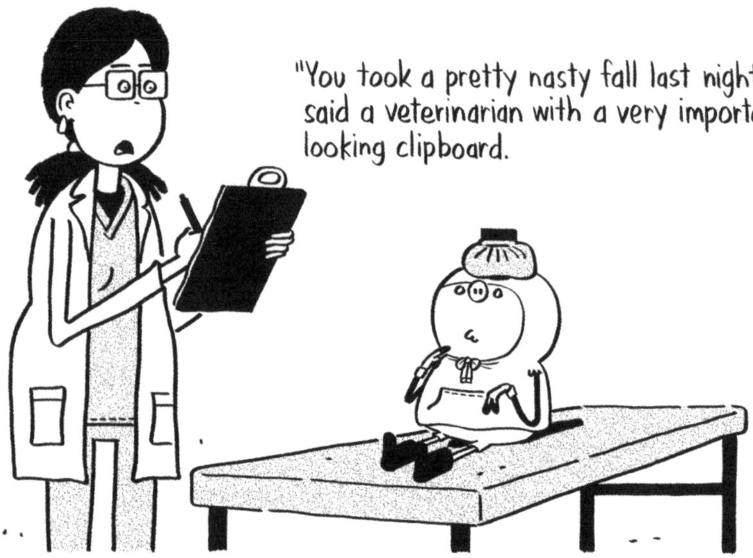

"But now let's talk about some important veterinarian stuff," said Dr. Pet Doctor. "I ran some tests and — as you can see on this x-ray — your insides are full of these LITTLE GUILTY FACES. Which means, Mr. Pigmund, you have A GUILT PROBLEM!"

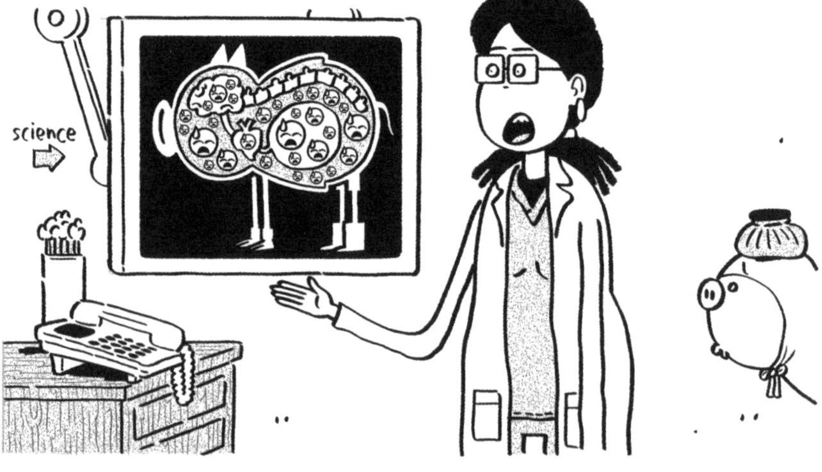
science

"Gasp! Oh NO! What does THAT mean?" said Chad, Lizárdo, and Mr. Buttercups.

"Well, from what I can piece together," said Dr. Pet Doctor. "I think Pigmund was feeling SO GUILTY about dragging his best friend Lizárdo into a scary new pet job that one day his brain just went — KABLOOEY! That's when your guilty conscience took over, Mr. Pigmund. You began dressing like a werewolf 'cause, deep down, you felt like A MONSTER."

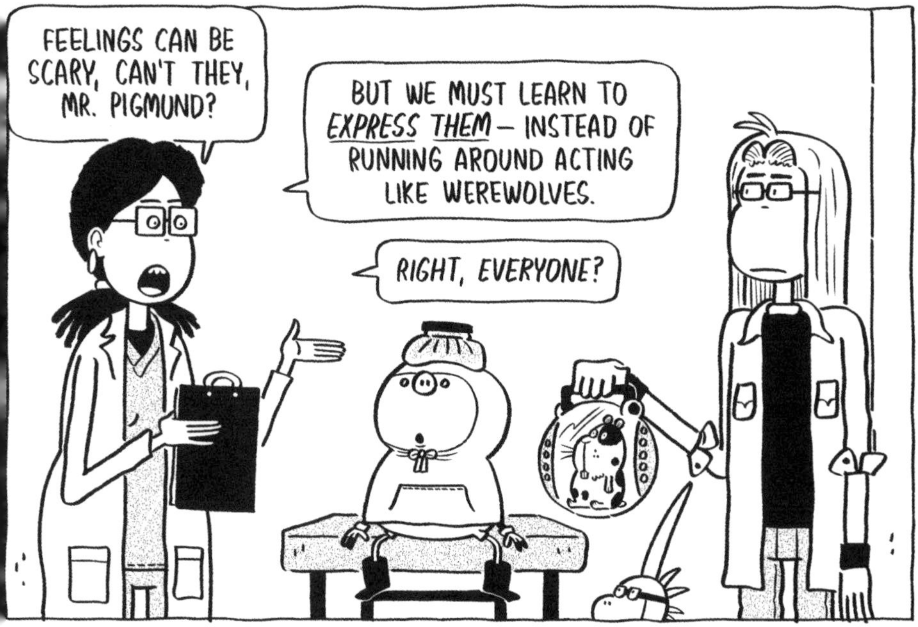
FEELINGS CAN BE SCARY, CAN'T THEY, MR. PIGMUND?
BUT WE MUST LEARN TO EXPRESS THEM — INSTEAD OF RUNNING AROUND ACTING LIKE WEREWOLVES.
RIGHT, EVERYONE?

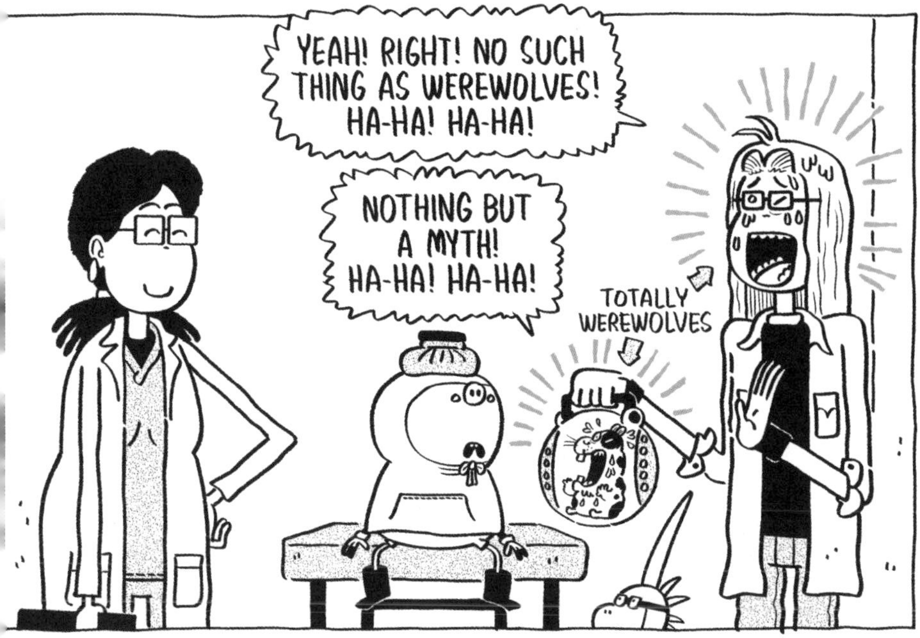
YEAH! RIGHT! NO SUCH THING AS WEREWOLVES! HA-HA! HA-HA!
NOTHING BUT A MYTH! HA-HA! HA-HA!
TOTALLY WEREWOLVES

Adventure 5

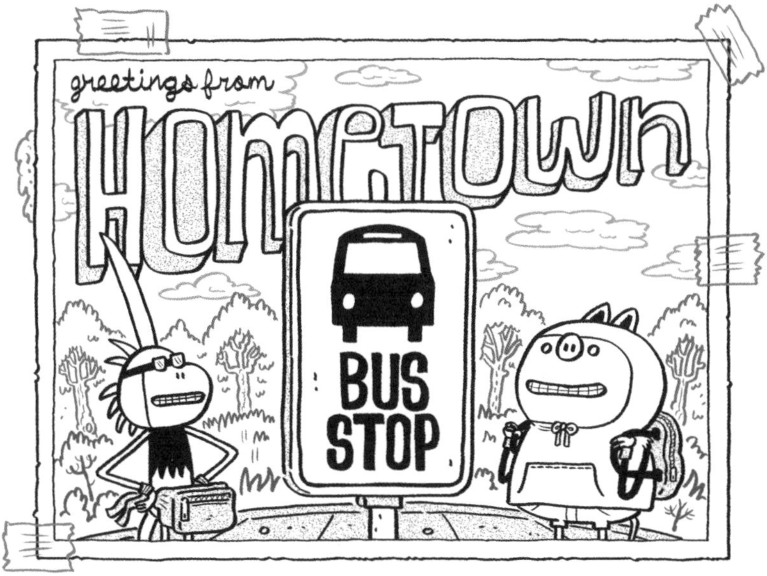
greetings from
HOMETOWN
BUS
STOP

Hello, Goodbyes

UNPETABLE AGAIN

AND SO — Dr. Pet Doctor released me from the hospital with three pats on the back and a Very Berry juice box.

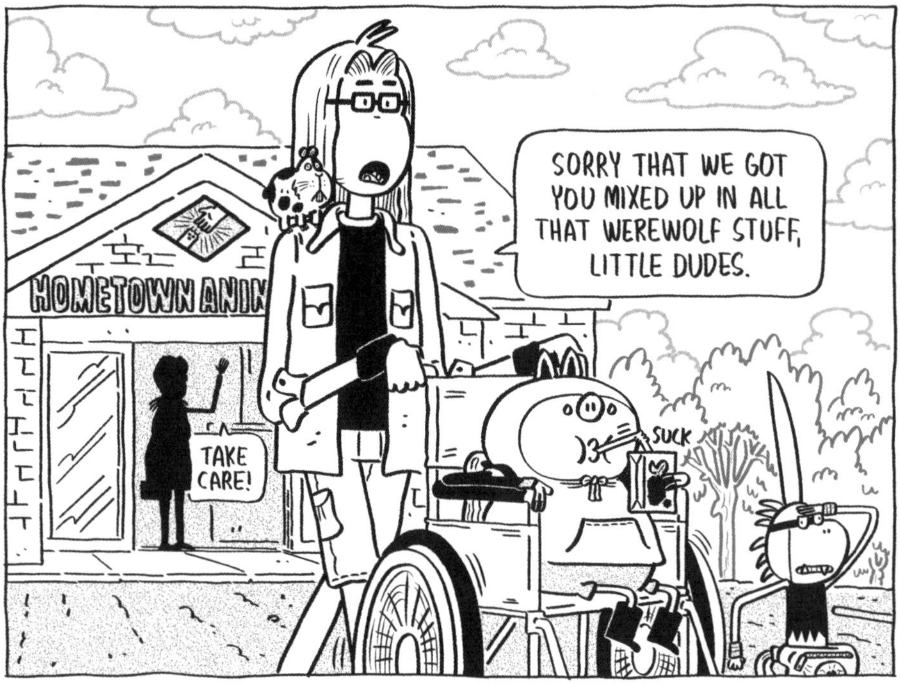
HOMETOWN ANIM
TAKE CARE!
SORRY THAT WE GOT YOU MIXED UP IN ALL THAT WEREWOLF STUFF, LITTLE DUDES.
SUCK

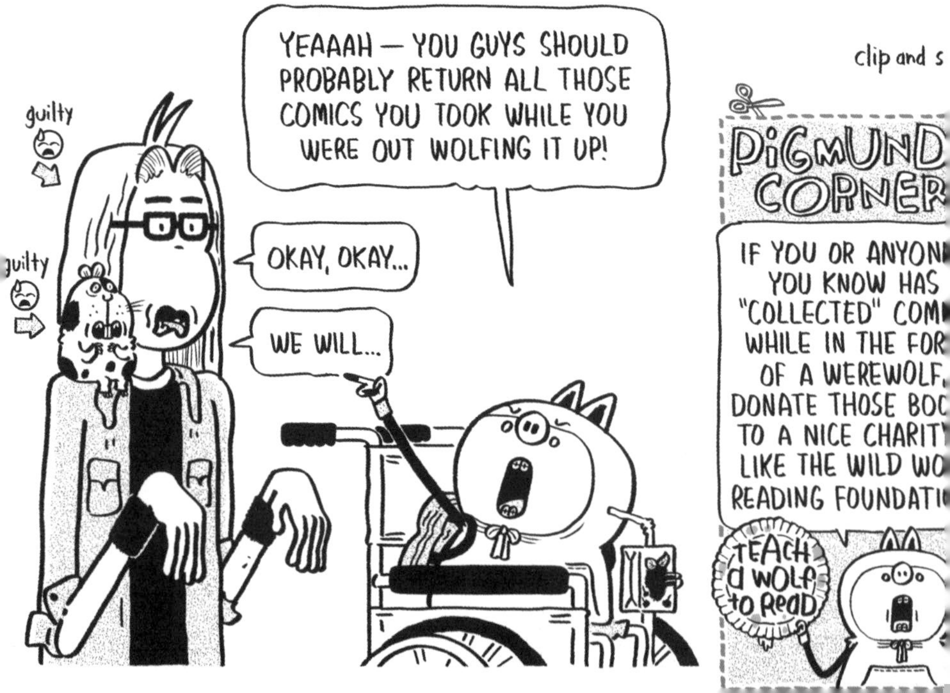
YEAAAH — YOU GUYS SHOULD PROBABLY RETURN ALL THOSE COMICS YOU TOOK WHILE YOU WERE OUT WOLFING IT UP!
guilty
guilty
OKAY, OKAY...
WE WILL...
clip and s
PIGMUND
CORNER
IF YOU OR ANYON
YOU KNOW HAS
"COLLECTED" COM
WHILE IN THE FOR
OF A WEREWOLF,
DONATE THOSE BOO
TO A NICE CHARIT
LIKE THE WILD WO
READING FOUNDATI
TEACH a WOLF to READ

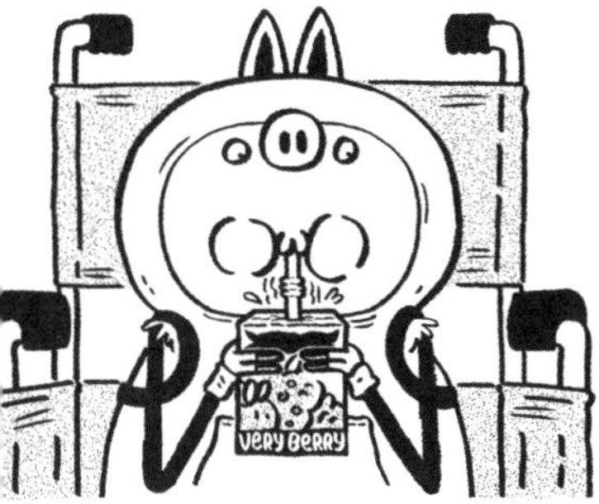
VERY BERRY

Which is when Lizárdo said:

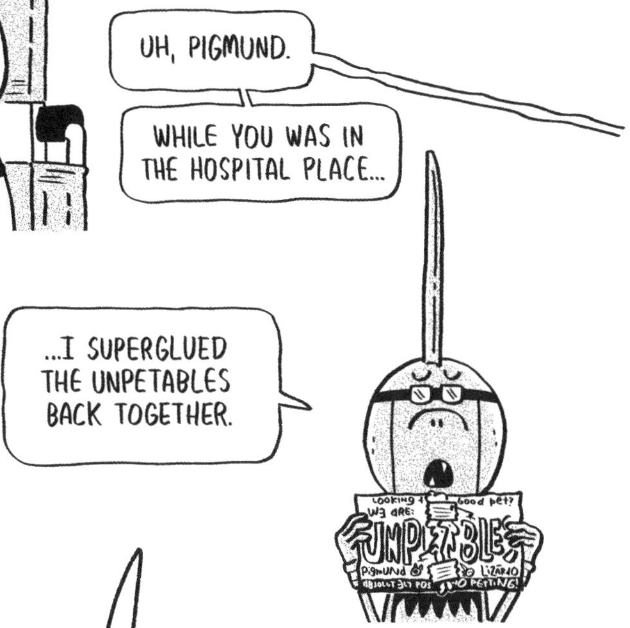
UH, PIGMUND.
WHILE YOU WAS IN THE HOSPITAL PLACE...
...I SUPERGLUED THE UNPETABLES BACK TOGETHER.

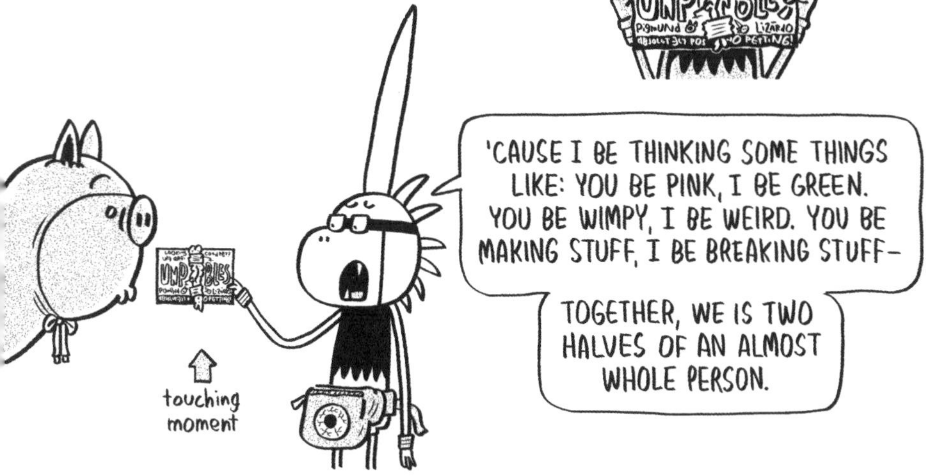
'CAUSE I BE THINKING SOME THINGS LIKE: YOU BE PINK, I BE GREEN. YOU BE WIMPY, I BE WEIRD. YOU BE MAKING STUFF, I BE BREAKING STUFF–
TOGETHER, WE IS TWO HALVES OF AN ALMOST WHOLE PERSON.
touching moment

I won't lie. Lizárdo's words made me feel ALL THE WARM FUZZIES.

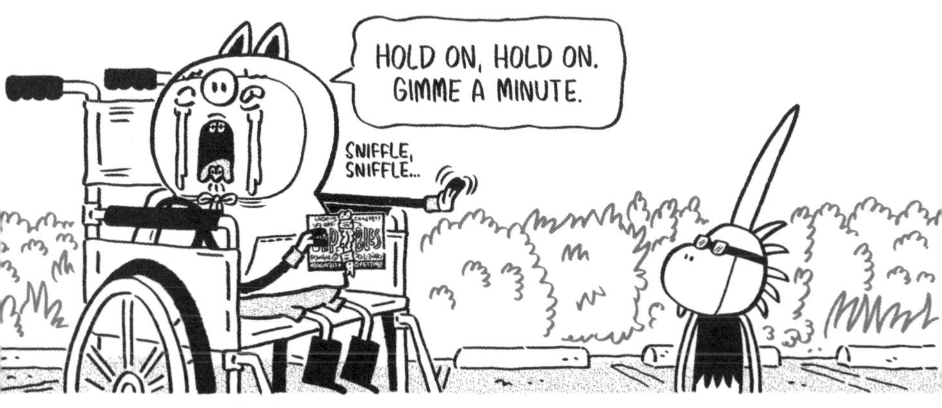
HOLD ON, HOLD ON. GIMME A MINUTE.
SNIFFLE, SNIFFLE...

"Chad, Mr. Buttercups," I said. "It's been super fun, but I think it's time for me and Lizárdo to MOVE ON. 'Cause there's a great big world out there, and the Unpetables have some candy to eat!"

"Yeah-yeah! CANDY-CANDY!"

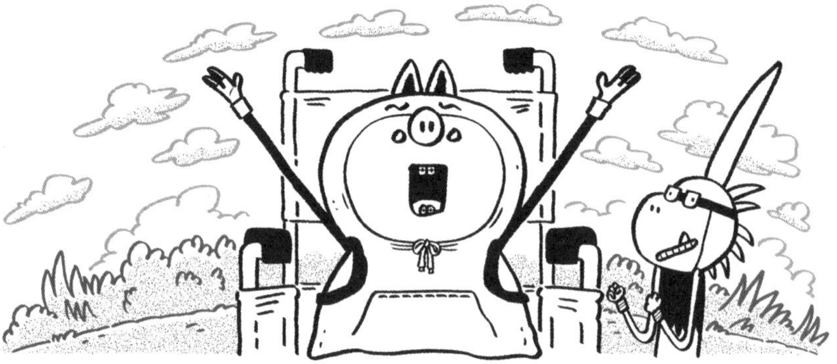

Which is EXACTLY when I got a GENIUS LEVEL idea.

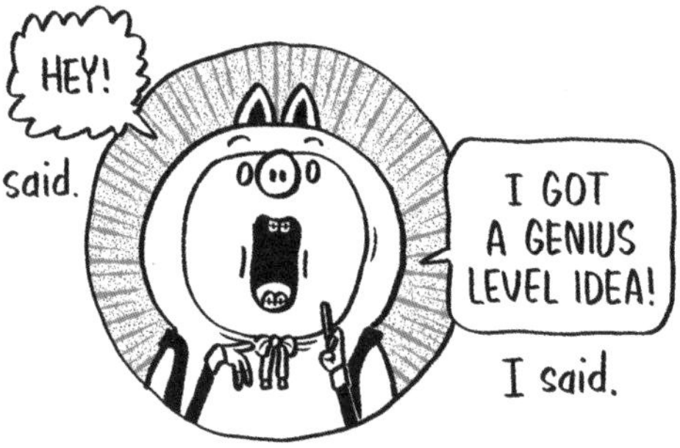
HEY!
I said.
I GOT A GENIUS LEVEL IDEA!
I said.

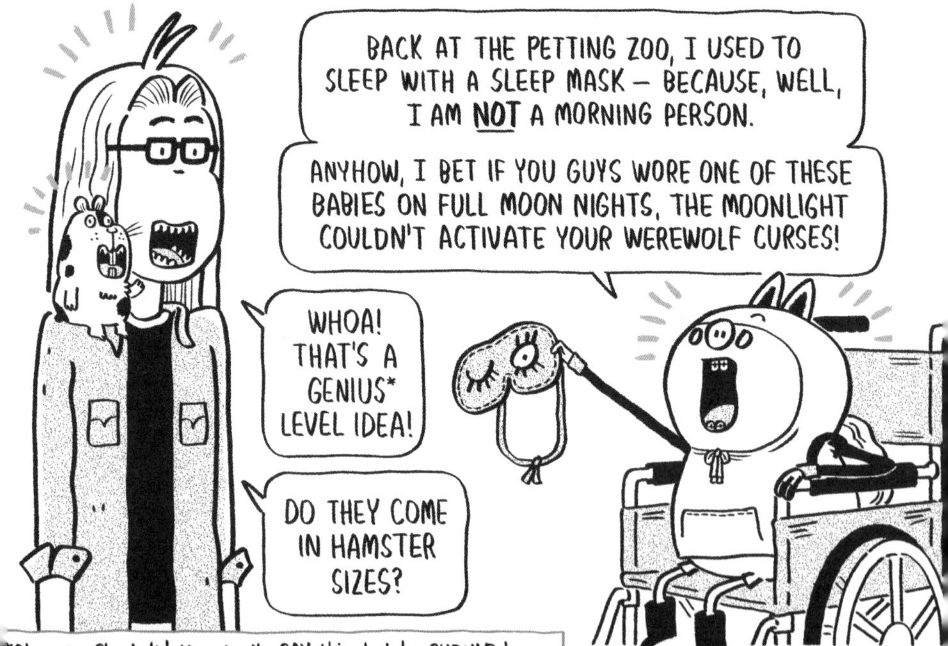
BACK AT THE PETTING ZOO, I USED TO SLEEP WITH A SLEEP MASK – BECAUSE, WELL, I AM NOT A MORNING PERSON.
ANYHOW, I BET IF YOU GUYS WORE ONE OF THESE BABIES ON FULL MOON NIGHTS, THE MOONLIGHT COULDN'T ACTIVATE YOUR WEREWOLF CURSES!
WHOA! THAT'S A GENIUS* LEVEL IDEA!
DO THEY COME IN HAMSTER SIZES?

*Okay, so Chad didn't actually SAY this, but he SHOULD have.

AND SO — having solved Chad and Mr. Buttercups' BIG, HAIRY problem, me and my best friend Lizárdo rolled off into the sun.

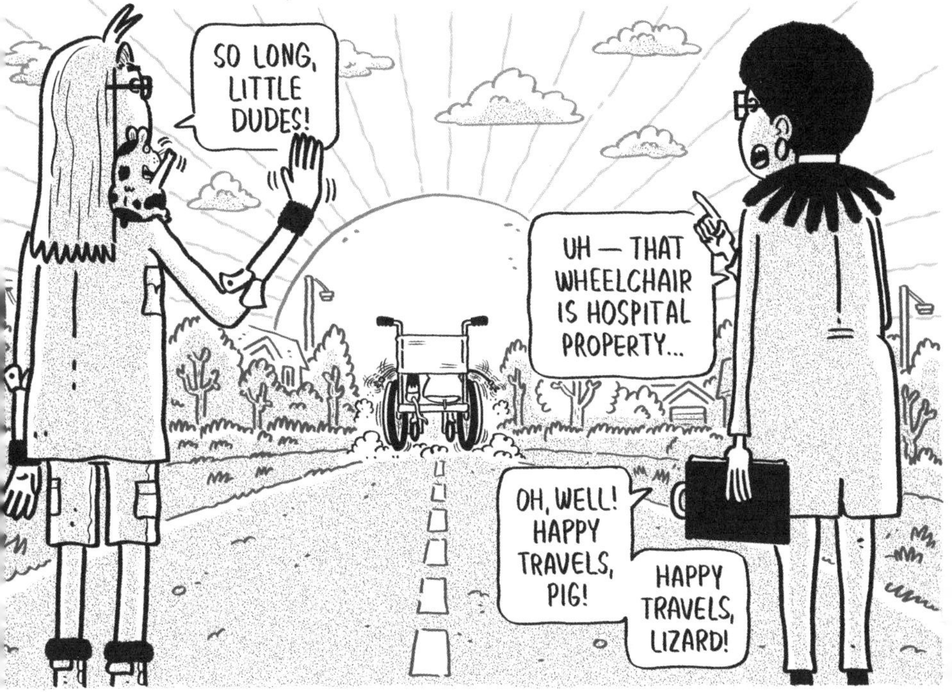
SO LONG, LITTLE DUDES!
UH — THAT WHEELCHAIR IS HOSPITAL PROPERTY...
OH, WELL! HAPPY TRAVELS, PIG!
HAPPY TRAVELS, LIZARD!

BUT — little did we know that Maintenance Man Kenny and his team of fluffy bunny suck-ups were hiding nearby — disguised as POTTED PLANTS.

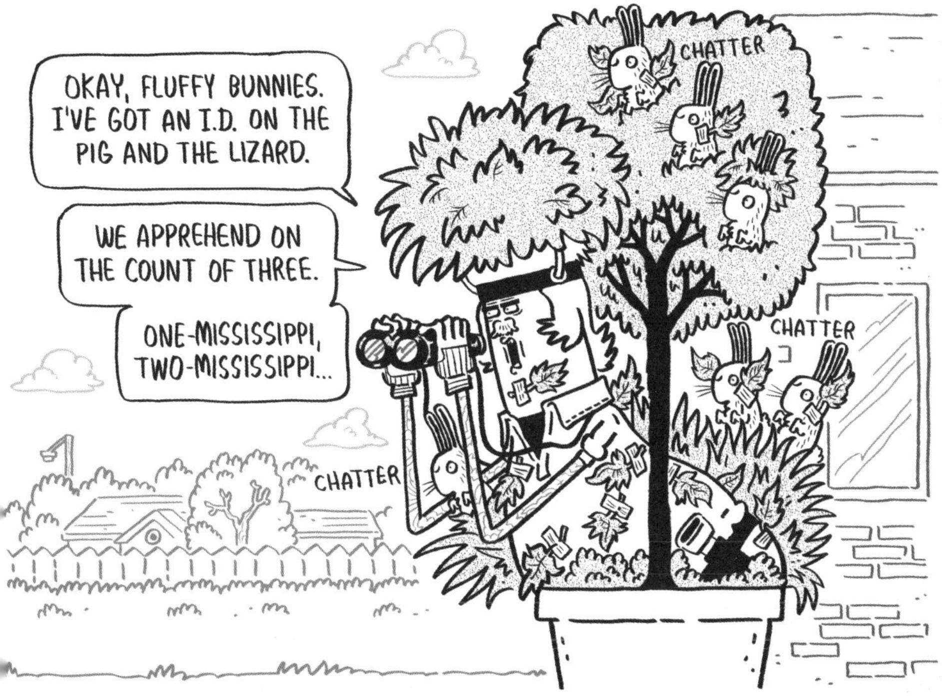
OKAY, FLUFFY BUNNIES. I'VE GOT AN I.D. ON THE PIG AND THE LIZARD.
CHATTER
WE APPREHEND ON THE COUNT OF THREE.
ONE-MISSISSIPPI, TWO-MISSISSIPPI...
CHATTER
CHATTER

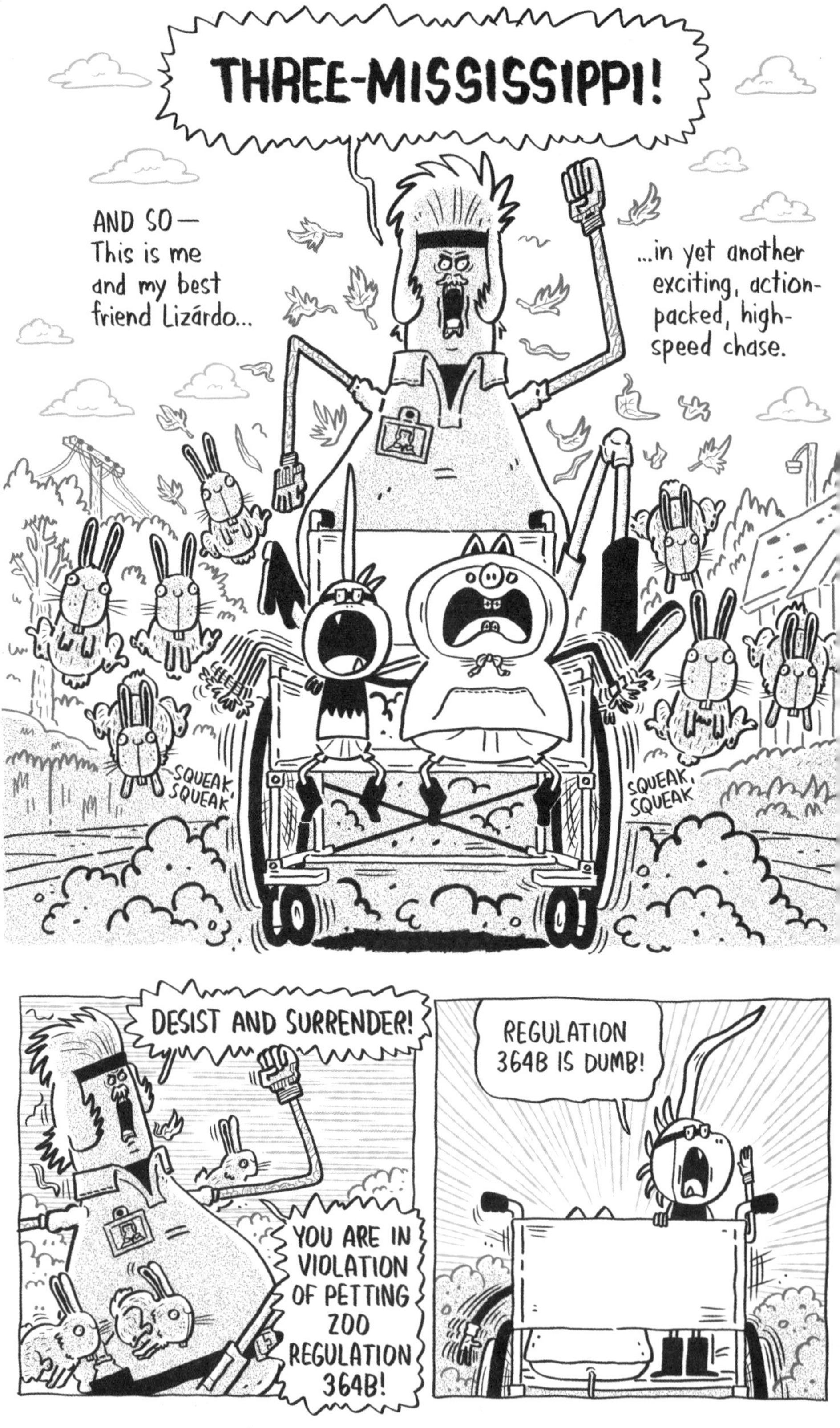
THREE-MISSISSIPPI!
AND SO— This is me and my best friend Lizárdo...
...in yet another exciting, action-packed, high-speed chase.
SQUEAK, SQUEAK
SQUEAK, SQUEAK
DESIST AND SURRENDER!
YOU ARE IN VIOLATION OF PETTING ZOO REGULATION 364B!
REGULATION 364B IS DUMB!

Some people call me A WIMP.

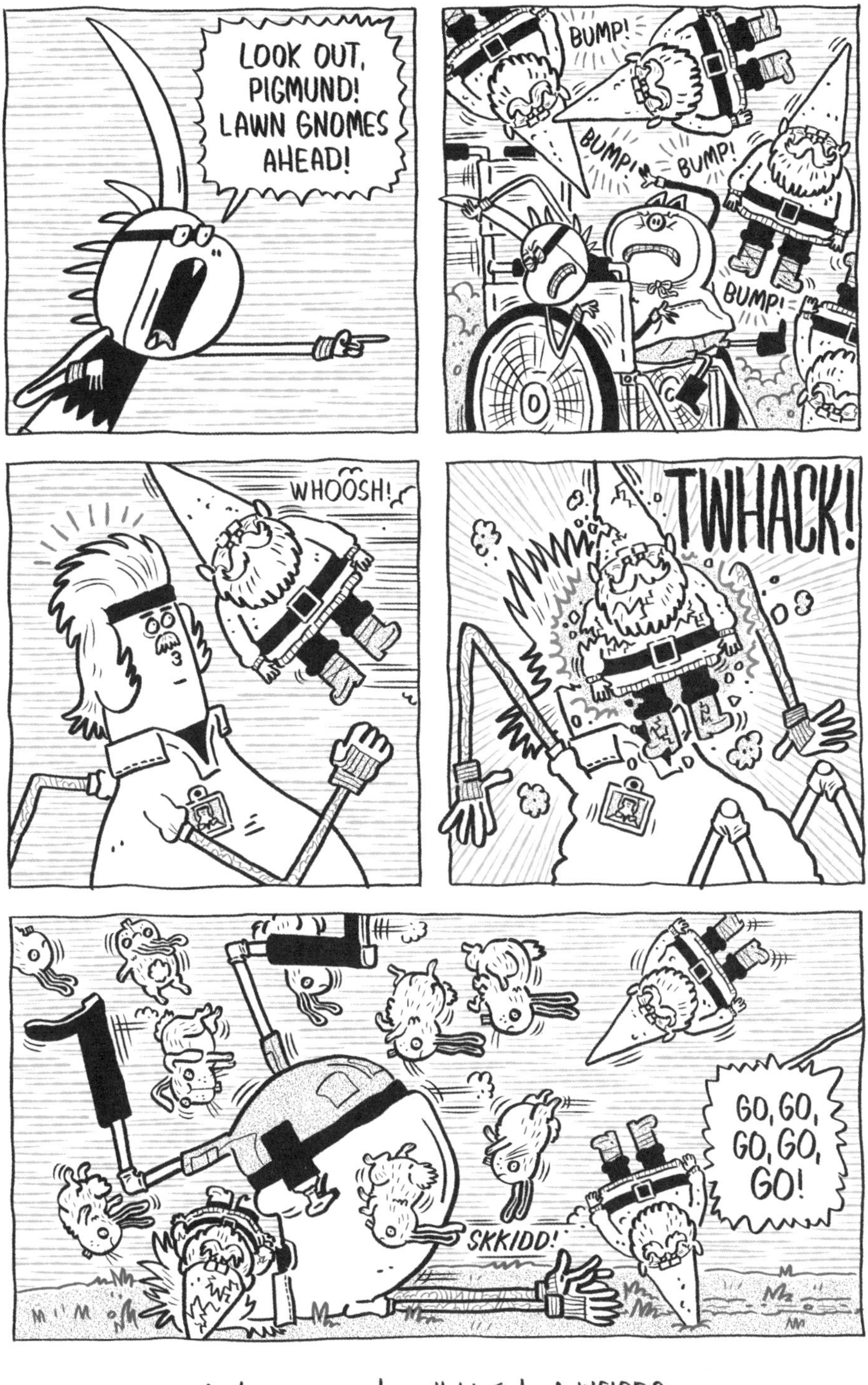
LOOK OUT, PIGMUND! LAWN GNOMES AHEAD!
BUMP!
BUMP!
BUMP!
BUMP!
WHOOSH!
TWHACK!
SKKIDD!
GO, GO, GO, GO, GO!

And some people call Lizárdo A WEIRDO.

But maybe,
JUST MAYBE...

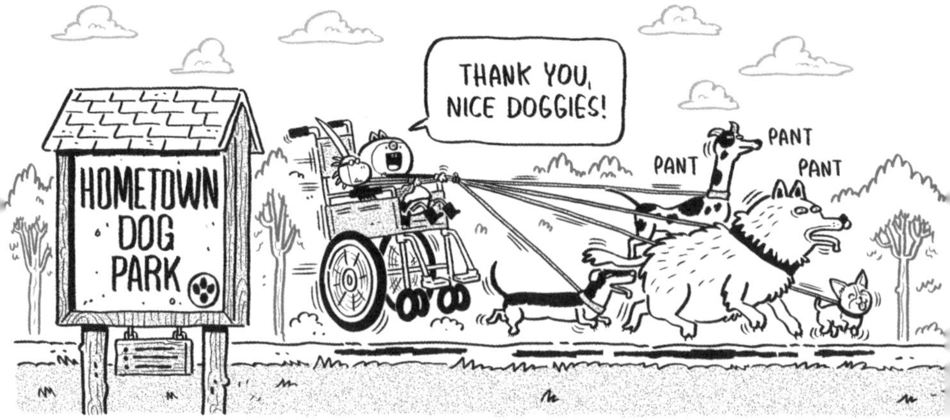
HOMETOWN DOG PARK
THANK YOU, NICE DOGGIES!
PANT
PANT
PANT

...it takes a WIMP
and a WEIRDO
to defeat the
MAINTENANCE MEN
of this world.

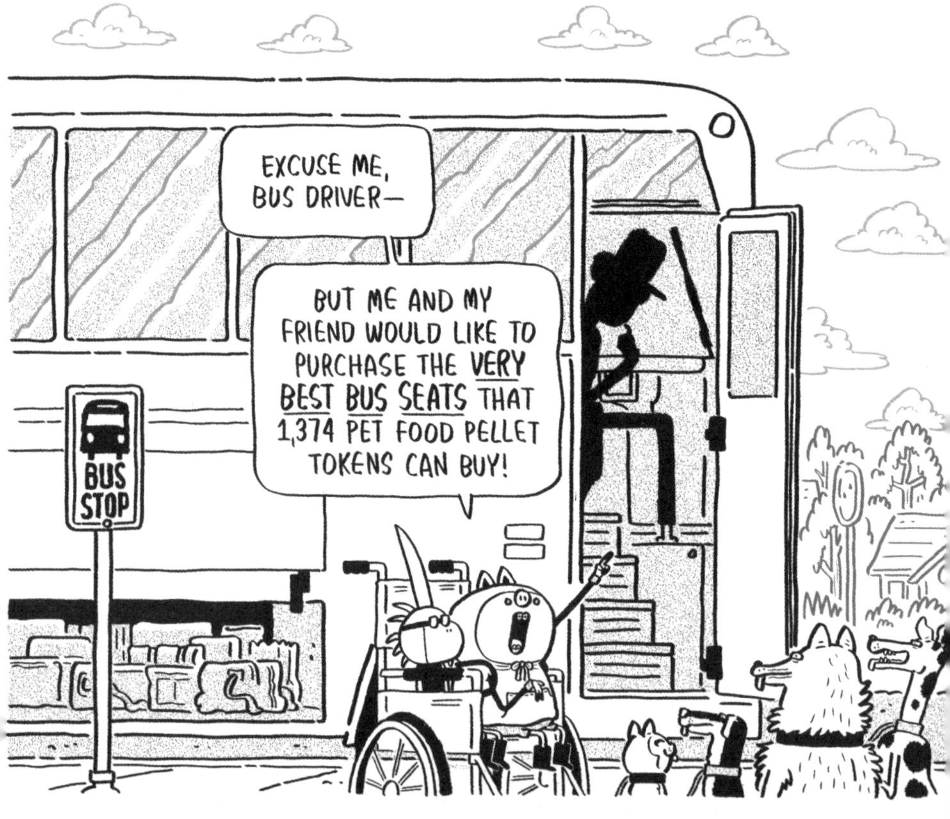
EXCUSE ME, BUS DRIVER—
BUT ME AND MY FRIEND WOULD LIKE TO PURCHASE THE VERY BEST BUS SEATS THAT 1,374 PET FOOD PELLET TOKENS CAN BUY!
BUS STOP

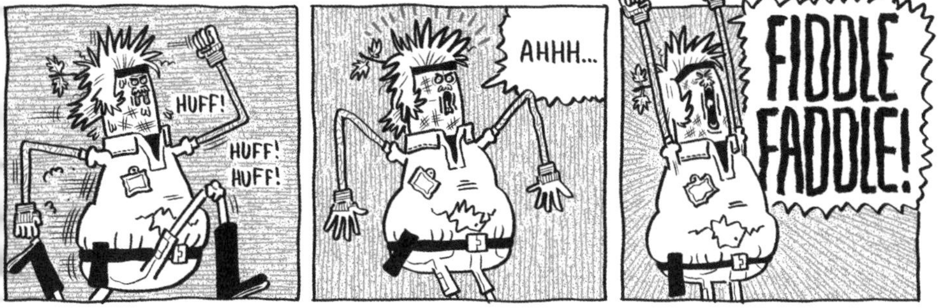
HUFF!
HUFF!
HUFF!
AHHH...
FIDDLE FADDLE!

AND SO—

if you're ever in need of a pet — on a strictly freelance basis, of course —just look around for me and my best friend Lizárdo.

We accept payments in cash, candy, and/or video game systems.

Love,
Sincerely,
Your pal,
Pigmund

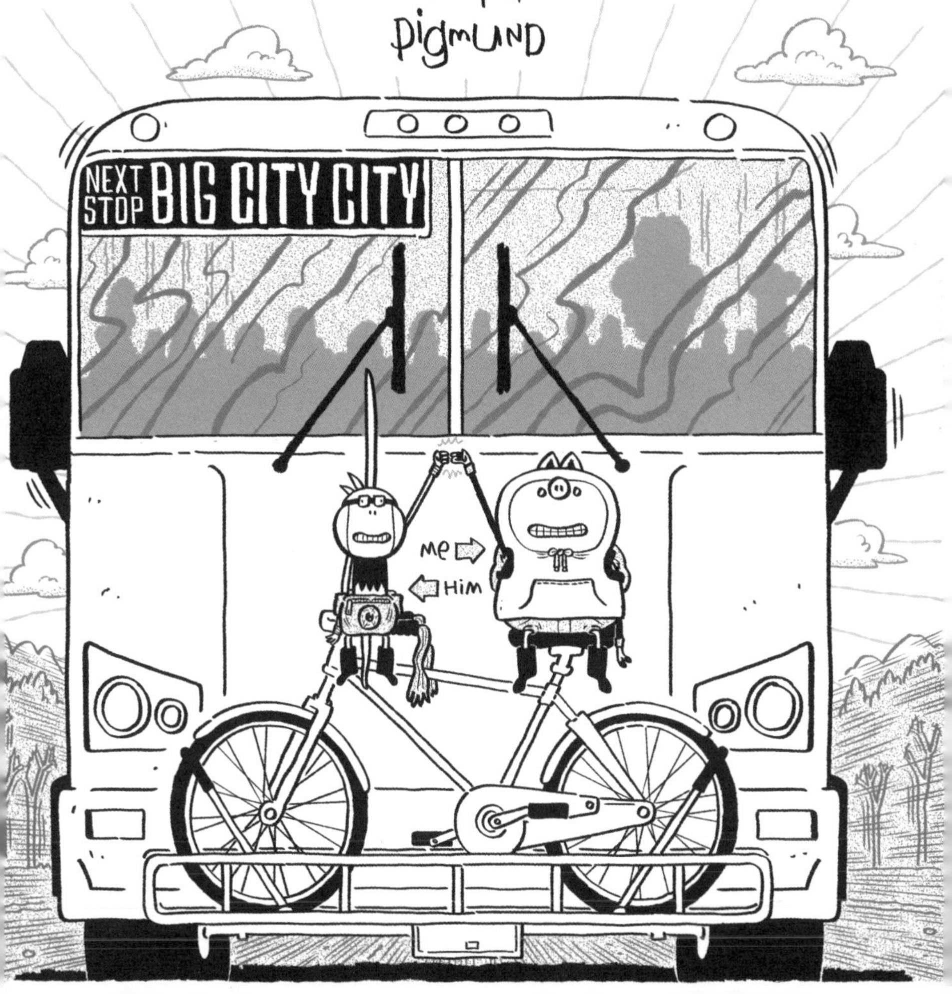
NEXT STOP BIG CITY CITY
Me
HIM

P.S.

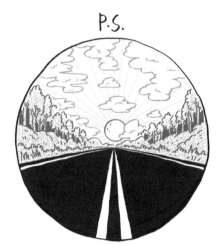

we are
UNPETABLE.

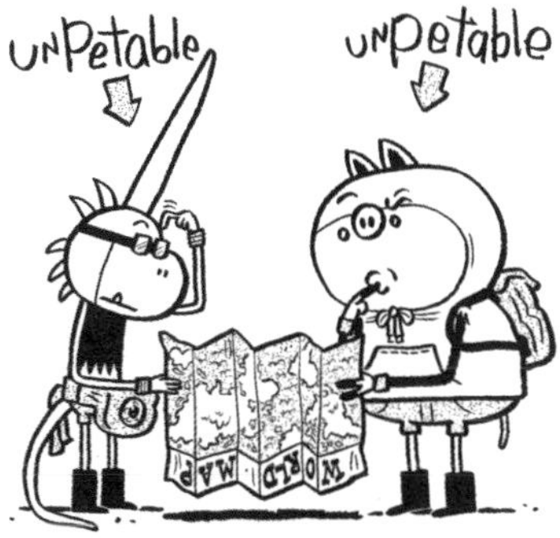
unPetable
unPetable
WORLD MAP

P.S. P.S.

Oh. And don't worry about Tiger and Stardust.
They got jobs as big, beautiful swans.

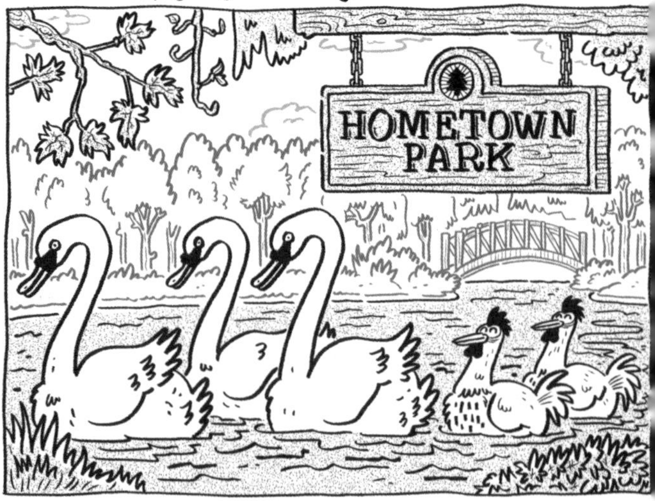
HOMETOWN
PARK